JACKSON

NEW HOPE SHIFTERS BOOK TWO

ELISA LEIGH

ELISA LEIGH ROMANCE

CONTENTS

CHAPTER 1

Waking up, I roll over in bed when I hear my phone go off. I'd like nothing more than to put my phone on silent and sleep in on my day off, but because of my job, I can't. As a police lieutenant, I have an obligation to my police chief and to this town. I have to be available at all hours, just in case there's an emergency. Luckily, there isn't much that goes on here besides the run of the mill goings-on of a small mountain town. As I've learned over the years, you never know what could happen, so I keep my eyes peeled for anything out of the ordinary. Anything that could harm the people of this town, or my pack.

Berkley Springs is a secluded town in the West Virginia mountains. One of the reasons we visited this town when we were trying to decide where our small pack should settle, was because of the low population and large amounts of forest land that surrounds the area. It's a quiet area where we can shift in privacy and live in peace. It was more than just this town that called to us though. Once my three cousins, brother, and I, stepped foot in town, a kind of knowing came over us. We all felt it in our bones that Berkley Springs was where we were supposed to be. This is where we would find our mates, even though no shifters lived in the area.

Grabbing my phone off of the nightstand, I see the missed call is from Jameson, my older brother, and the Alpha of our pack. It's then that I see it's already ten-thirty in the morning. I can't believe I slept this late. Usually, I wake up between five-thirty and six on the weekends and will go for a run around our property, but I had a hard time falling asleep last night. Jameson and Lillian hosted a game night for our pack yesterday. This is usually where Lillian tries out her recipes on us. For the most part, they've all turned out great, except for when she tried making sushi. I love sushi, but Lillian's did not turn out well. They kept things easy last night and made frozen pizzas while we played poker.

When I got home from Jameson's, I devoured the rest of the Tom Clancy novel I had been reading. After I finished the book, I tried going to sleep, but I kept thinking about my life here in Berkley Springs. The main thing that kept running through my head is how lonely I feel here, which I shouldn't since I'm doing what I love and living close to my best friends. It's too hard to see Jameson and Lillian together. I'm happy for him, I really am, but it hurts, physically hurts, knowing he has the very thing I desire, a mate. It's not fair to anyone that I feel this way and the last thing I want is to take away from their happiness. I'm going to tell Jameson that I'm considering moving back home. I'm about to call Jameson back when he sends me a text message.

Jameson: I need to talk to you. Are you working right now?
Me: No, I'm off today. What's up?
Jameson: Want to come over for breakfast?
Me: Sure, I'll be over in twenty minutes. There's something I want to talk to you about too.
Jameson: See you then.

After I've showered, I shift into my bear and run over to my brother's home which is only a two-minute drive down the road and maybe five minutes in my bear. I make sure to grab my bag of clothes to change into before I take off. When we bought the sixty-acre property, we designed it so that everyone had an equal share. The property is surrounded by a ten-foot-high wrought iron fence. To get in you need to scan your fingerprint or use the call box for someone to let you in. We don't have access codes, that way, no one can hack into the security system. A single paved road goes from the gate and up along the property line, although a twenty-foot barrier between the fence and the road is covered in tall trees. There's a good reason for all of our security measures, one we don't like remembering.

I make sure to knock and wait for someone to answer the door before walking in. The last time I walked in without knocking I found Jameson and Lillian naked in the kitchen. Jameson about tore me to shreds for that mistake. I think his bear was even more pissed than he was and took it out on me the next time we all went for a run in our bear form. I understand where he's coming from though, if I ever find my mate there's no way in hell, I'd want anyone but me seeing her naked. Since then, I always knock.

Lillian opens the door smiling brightly up at me. She's a beautiful girl but today she looks like she's glowing.

"Good morning Jackson!" She says giving me a warm hug.

I hug my sister-in-law tight and that's when I realize something has changed. Her scent is different than it used to be.

When she pulls away, she walks ahead of me as I close the door and follow after her.

"Jameson is in his office talking to the hospital about one of his patients. Can I get you a cup of coffee?"

"I can get it Lil, why don't you sit down, I know where everything is," I say not wanting her to have to wait on me.

She waves me off and opens a cabinet to get a plate down. "I made a breakfast casserole this morning, would you like some?"

"Is that what smells so damn good?" I ask making her smile.

"Stop flirting with my mate," Jameson says walking into the kitchen. He wraps his arm around Lillian's side and tugs her close.

The connection they share through their mating bond is something I yearn for. I try not to let my smile slip when he inhales her scent and drops a kiss on the side of her head.

"I'll take a piece too, sweetheart, if you don't mind," Jameson tells her. "Not at all." She says grabbing another plate from the cabinet. He kisses her lips then walks to their large dining room table that could easily seat twelve.

Giving up on making my own plate, I take a seat next to Jameson at the table. Lillian moves around the kitchen with ease as she plates up some breakfast casserole and warms it in the microwave.

"How is it going, Jackie?" Jameson asks, calling me by the nickname he gave me when we were kids. He doesn't use it often, but when he does, I know he's talking to me as a brother and not as my Alpha.

"Going alright, I guess."

He gives me a concerned look. Being only three years younger than him, he's spent over fifty years as my brother and knows when I'm not being honest with him. "I haven't really had a chance to talk to you lately. Anything new going on down at the station?" He asks.

I take a sip of my coffee, enjoying how the hot liquid coats my throat and helps to perk me up. "Not really. You know nothing ever goes on around here."

Jameson smirks and knocks his knuckles against the dark wood table twice. "And that's how I like it."

"How about at the hospital?" I ask.

He shrugs, but I can tell something is bothering him. "The days change, but it's just a lot of the same. People don't pay attention to what they're doing, and they hurt themselves, or worse..." He says then looks over at his wife.

I'm sure he's thinking about how he met Lillian over six months ago. She came into the Emergency Room close to death and he had to save her, all while just finding out that she was his mate.

Lillian comes walking out of the kitchen with two plates piled high with breakfast casserole and some fruit salad. She sets a plate down in front of each of us and my mouth waters as I inhale the delicious scent of the meal.

"Lil, this smells incredible. Thank you."

Standing next to Jameson, she wraps her arm over his shoulder and looks at me with a giant smile. "You're welcome, Jackson. You know I love cooking for my family."

Guilt hits me in the chest for the thoughts I've had as of late. Lillian and Jameson were married, shortly after they were mated, in a simple ceremony down at the courthouse. It was such a spur of the moment event that only our cousins and I attended. Lillian didn't care though, she said her family was there and that's all that mattered to her. I think being a part of our family and our pack has helped to heal those parts of her heart that for so long went abandoned. Since then, Lillian has helped bring the pack even closer together. She's always planning game nights or bonfires, something so that we can all be together. She missed out on that growing up and is making up for it now. None of us mind, we love being together.

Lillian clears her throat and I look up to see that she's now sitting across from me holding Jameson's hand. "Jameson and I wanted you to be the first to know."

My brows pull together. "To know what?" I ask and look over at my brother who is staring at his wife.

"We're pregnant!" She bursts.

I watch as Jameson stares longingly at his wife with love and devotion. Damn, that must really be something. Another pang of guilt mixed with jealousy hits me in the gut.

"Congratulations. I'm so happy for you two."

Lillian squeals with excitement. "Isn't it amazing? In less than nine months we're going to have a little cub in our pack."

For a human, she's adapted to her mating, and shifter life in general, better than I expected. Human-shifter matings are rare, but they happen.

I realize she doesn't have food in front of her. "Why aren't you eating?"

"Oh, I ate earlier, I couldn't wait. I'm also meeting a friend for lunch in about an hour. Speaking of..." She checks her watch then immediately stands. "Oh shoot! I need to change."

She rushes out of the room to go get ready and I can't help but laugh.

I love my sister-in-law as if she were my sister and I worry about her leaving the property without one of us with her. "Who is she having lunch with?"

"Hannah."

I take a bite of the breakfast casserole and am not disappointed. "Did Lillian make this?"

Jameson nods his head while shoveling large bites into his mouth.

While I'm eating, I wrack my brain trying to remember if she's ever mentioned Hannah to me before, but I can't remember. I know that before the accident, Lillian didn't have many friends.

"Hannah who?"

"She's a nurse that works with me at the hospital. She's good people Jackson, I wouldn't let her be around someone who would hurt her."

"I know, it's just... you never know what people's intentions are."

He nods. "They were good friends in high school but lost touch. They met again when Lillian was in the hospital and reconnected. Lillian and she hang out a few times a month and have become really close. She's been over here for a couple of family dinners, I'm surprised you haven't met her yet."

Knowing she's been here shouldn't irritate the shit out of me, but it does. A stranger has been spending time with my family and I didn't even know about it. How much time have I been spending away from my pack? I know I've been picking up a lot of overtime lately at work, mostly to stay away from Lillian and Jameson. I'm a shitty brother and brother-in-law.

"Hey, I'm sure you'll meet her soon enough."

I smile tightly. This shit has gone on long enough. I need to make a decision, one that isn't going to hurt my family. If I stay, my bitterness could rub off on everyone else, but if I go, I won't be here to see my niece or nephew grow up. I wish I could talk to Jameson about this, but I can't, not about this. Weston would probably understand better than anyone. If he can handle it, I sure as hell can.

Lillian comes walking back up to the table and gives Jameson a kiss on the cheek. "I have to go or I'm going to be late."

Jameson stands. "I'll walk you out."

"I'm going to go too," I say and stand with my plate in my hand. I grab Jameson's plate and take them to the sink with my coffee cup and rinse them out. I meet them at the door where they're sharing a heated kiss.

I clear my throat and they pull away from each other,

Lillian with bright red cheeks and Jameson glaring at me for interrupting.

"Oh Jackson, before I forget, we're all getting together Friday night to celebrate the pregnancy as a pack. I really hope you'll be able to make it."

"I'll be there, Lil. I promise."

CHAPTER 2

HANNAH FINNIGAN

I'm waiting outside Bella Cafe, a new restaurant that opened up recently, for Lillian to show up. Lillian suggested this place to me the other day because of the all you can drink mimosas they offer on Sundays. We're meeting up for lunch and to hopefully do a little shopping afterward. Now that I'm making good money as a nurse, I've decided to splurge and find a few new outfits since most of my clothes have come from second-hand shops and are worn out.

Ever since Lillian's accident back in January, we have been spending a lot of time together. We went over seven years without talking and it hurt when I lost her. I understand why she pulled away, especially now since she's opened up more about what she dealt with after her father's death. Her brother is an asshole and I want nothing more than to beat him over his pathetic head for how he treated Lillian. I was happy when she finally put her foot down and told him to get himself cleaned up if he wanted any kind of relationship with her. I'm just happy to have my best friend back in my life.

When my dad left my mom and me, we moved to Berkley Springs, West Virginia to live with my grandma. She was going through cancer treatments and needed someone to help take care of her and we needed to leave town. As a sophomore in high school, it was really hard finding people to talk to. A lot of people our age already had friends since they all grew up together in this small town. Lillian was the only person who made an effort to get to know me. We were just two misfit teen girls trying to make it through the turbulent seas of high school. That year wasn't easy, but Lillian made the transition easier and was a friend when I needed one. I'll always be grateful to her.

"Sorry, sorry. Jackson came over later than I thought and then I lost track of time." Lillian says walking up to me quickly. When she finally gets to me, she gives me a fast but warm hug.

"No worries. I was only waiting out here for a few minutes." I tell her, hugging her back.

Once we're seated, I look over the menu liking the mimosa options they have available. "I think I'm going to get the pineapple coconut mimosa, which one are you going to try?" I ask.

"The kind without champagne."

I look up from the menu and quirk my brow at my best friend. "What? Why? The champagne is the best part."

She gives me a big toothy grin. "I can't have alcohol for at least 9 months."

"You're pregnant?" I shout.

She nods eagerly. "Yes! Can you believe it? I took a test this morning. I was so nervous it would be negative again, but Jameson encouraged me to take it. I'm still in shock that it was positive!"

I stand and give her the biggest hug I can manage. "I'm so happy for you Lillian. I know you two have been trying to get pregnant for a while now."

When I sit back down and look back at my friend, she's smiling like nothing could steal her joy. What I wouldn't give to have a love like that in my life. Men like Jameson Walker are rare, rarer than rare, and my friend was lucky enough to find one. I can't help the tinge of jealousy that sparks inside my chest seeing her this happy.

If you want what Lillian has you need to give love a shot, I think to myself. I've never given dating a real go of it. Sure, there were the boys in middle school who asked me to be their girlfriends, but those were harmless crushes on silly boys. After my father left us for another woman, to start a family with her three kids, anger like I've never known before grew inside me. How dare he leave me and my mom, to trade one family for another. What was it about us that wasn't good enough for him?

I shake my head trying to clear the ugly memories

from my mind. This isn't about me, it's about Lillian. I'm not going to ruin this for her.

"Will you be able to come?"

"Huh?" I ask focusing on Lillian.

She laughs. "I said, will you be able to make it to the bonfire we're having on Friday?"

For a split second, I think to tell her no, wanting to wallow in my self-pity rather than celebrate her bundle of joy. I'm not that much of a bitch though and I really am happy for her and Jameson. "Of course, I'll be there. What should I bring?"

Lillian waves me off. "Girl, you don't have to bring anything."

I give her a look and she rolls her eyes. "Remington and Hudson will be grilling steaks and burgers. I'll be making potato salad and seven-layer bean dip. Do you want to bring a dessert?"

"You got it, Lil. I'll make sure to bring plenty. I know how much those guys can eat." I laugh remembering the last time I was over to hang out with Lillian for one of her infamous game nights. Jameson's cousin Hudson came walking into their house with ten pizzas. I was sure there were more people showing up, but Lillian assured me it was just us. I was amazed the guys ate over two pizzas a piece and still looked hungry.

Just then our waiter walks over to take our order and Lillian happily orders an orange juice while I ask for the pineapple coconut mimosa.

It's Friday night and I just finished my last of four twelve-hour shifts this morning at seven o'clock. When I got home, I took a hot shower and crawled into bed exhausted and ready to sleep most of my day away. Thankfully, I'll be off for the next three days. Since I'm a newbie at the hospital, I got stuck working the graveyard shift. I don't mind it most of the time, but that also means I'm forced to work with Dr. Hammond. The guy skeeves me out. I've heard so many stories about how he makes the other female nurses feel uncomfortable. I've tried keeping my distance not wanting to fall prey to his unwanted interest. It worked for a while, but lately, he's sought me out to ask me questions about his patients, the information he could have gotten if he would just read their charts. He hasn't done anything that I could take to Human Resources, but if he tries crossing the line, I'm ready to put him in his place. I won't put up with anyone taking advantage of me, especially a man. It sickens me to know that he's gotten away with this behavior for so long. If it costs me my job so be it, there are plenty of other hospitals in this country and it would give me the push I need to leave this town and move on with my life. I'd hate to leave Lillian behind now that we just started talking again.

I get maybe six hours of sleep before I wake up and I'm ready to get my day started. Usually, on my first day off I'll sleep until four or five in the afternoon. I've never been one of those people who can stay in bed for a while playing on my phone. I need to get up and have my coffee, even if it is the middle of the afternoon, and make my list of things I need to get done today.

After the first sip of java hits my tongue I groan in relief. There really is nothing like that first hit of coffee after you wake up. I go sit down at my desk and take another sip of coffee before I grab my notepad and my favorite dark blue sparkly gel pen. At the top of the paper, I write TO DO TODAY in all caps. Tapping the bottom of the pen against my lip I think about what I want and need to do. I definitely need to hit the grocery store to stock up on basics. My refrigerator is bare except for a few eggs, some outdated milk, some leftover Chinese takeout, coffee creamer, and condiments. I also need to grab all of the ingredients for my peanut butter chocolate trifle and corn casserole for tonight's bonfire at Lillian's. I know she said to bring dessert, but I feel like we'll definitely need more food with the way those men can put it away. It's crazy how they can eat the way they do and still look like Greek gods. Jameson and all of his cousins are muscular and good looking, just like him, but I have no interest in any of them. To me, they feel like a brother would.

I write my list, adding grocery shopping, laundry, pay bills, and make food for tonight. Reading over my list, I'm happy with it, but I have this nagging feeling. Have I missed something? I walk to my room and grab my phone off the charger and pull up my calendar. There's nothing going on today or the rest of the month, except for my dad's birthday at the end of the month. I should get a card to send out to him, I think and snort. Did I really just think about sending my dad a card?

Ever since my parents' divorce, it was court mandated that I spend at least a month during the summer and one holiday with him. The first time I went I pretty much ignored him and his wife Juanita. I didn't want to like her and hated her on principle. She was the reason my parents were no longer together. By the end of the summer, I still hadn't said much to her or my dad. Juanita's three kids who were three, seven, and nine were the exception. They were so stinking cute. The first time I hurt one of their feelings I felt it down in my soul, I couldn't be that person. It wasn't their fault their mom did what she did. From then on, every time I came to visit, I spent most of my time with the kids and was civil with Dad and Juanita.

What the heck is wrong with me these days, I keep thinking about the past. It's not like I can do anything about it now. To Juanita's credit, she was never mean to me. If anything, she was overly nice, even though I didn't deserve it. I was a shit to her at first.

After making a grocery list and paying my bills, I get up and go get ready for my day, throwing on a pair of jean shorts and a baseball-style three-quarter length tee. I put my beloved Cubs baseball cap on my head to hide my wild strawberry blonde waves and leave for the grocery store.

By the time I get back home and put my groceries away

I have just enough time to get the trifle made and put in the fridge to set up while I make the corn casserole and get ready. I get distracted by looking at Facebook for a while and end up rushing to finish the casserole and get ready. I stare at myself in the mirror for a split second trying to decide what to wear. Pulling my hair out of its ponytail, I run my fingers through my long wavy hair. I should probably get a trim soon since it's been almost a year. I shrug, not caring how I look since it's just Lillian, Jameson, and his cousins, I put on my most comfortable ratty pair of jeans, flip flops and a white tank top. I grab my Cubs hoodie in case it gets cold and run out the door almost forgetting the food.

Rushing to get there, I'm not paying attention once I pull onto their property. I'm almost to Lillian's when a giant bear runs out in front of my car. I slam on my breaks barely missing him. The giant bear stares at me with large golden-brown eyes. With my heart just about beating out of my chest, I lean my head against my steering wheel to catch my breath. When I look up to see if the bear is still there, I see it running off into the woods. It's dark, but I swear I see it stop and look back at me. Something crazy happens in that instant. The nagging that I've been feeling all day is gone and a warm feeling starts to spread over me.

I drive the rest of the way to Lillian and Jameson's place and park next to Lillian's Jeep. I don't bother grabbing the food, telling myself I'll go back for it in a few minutes.

"Oh my God you guys, I almost hit a freaking bear!" I

shout when I walk into Lillian's back door that leads directly into the kitchen.

Everyone stops what they're doing in the kitchen and stares at me, everyone but Lillian who is grinning like a loon.

CHAPTER 3

Notes of cinnamon and vanilla waft through the air and my bear takes notice lifting his nose to inhale the scent. Breathing in traces of wildflowers and a sweet woodsy aroma gives me the feeling of home, more than I've ever felt. That's when I realize I've scented her. I've scented my mate.

Mate.

My bear takes off, running as fast as he can go to get to her before she disappears. The woman we have been waiting for is finally within reach and we won't let her get away. I break through the trees and run into the road, stopping when what I've been chasing my entire life is before me. A white car comes to a screeching halt, inches from my bear.

It's hard to see her face since she's in her car, but what I can see has me captivated. My bear is pushing for me to go to her, to claim her, but I hold him back because shining back at me are her bright blue eyes, open wide in shock. When she looks away, I run off towards my house to change quickly. My bear doesn't like it and makes it known, roaring as I push him forward and away from our mate. He's worried she'll get away from us, but I know better. *We'll be with her in a few minutes. If she's on the property that means someone must have let her in. There's no way she was able to get in any other way. Give me a minute to change. We can't go to her as a bear and risk her leaving because she doesn't understand us.* I tell my bear, needing him to calm down. I pray for my cousins' sakes she's here for Lillian and not any of them. My bear strongly agrees.

When I pull up to Jameson's home all of the vehicles look familiar except one. Jameson's truck is parked on the right of Lillian's black Jeep that he got her a few weeks after her accident. On the other side of Jameson are Hudson and Weston's trucks. Remington probably caught a ride with his twin Hudson. None of that matters to me right now though, because all the way at the other end of the row of vehicles, parked next to Lillian's Jeep, is a white Camry.

Bingo! A slow smile spreads across my face. It's the very same white Camry that almost hit me not ten minutes ago.

I purposely park beside her and get out of my truck. I'm dying to get in there and meet my mate, but before I do, I check out her car. Something is bothering me about it. Call it police intuition or shifter senses, I can't leave until I've inspected it. Thankful for my shifter abilities, I'm able to check out her car in the low setting sun. The car looks to be almost twenty years old and is in rough condition. I sniff around her car, smelling chocolate and some other kind of food making my stomach rumble, whatever it is, I want it. My bear gnashes his teeth when we realize there's another scent that isn't her own. It comes from a male, someone unrelated to her. Who has been in her car? Anger surges through me hoping to hell she isn't taken by another man. Whoever he is, he won't be in her life any longer. My bear settles, liking where my head is at.

Not finding anything that raises any red flags, besides the male scent, I make my way into the house. Before opening the back door to the kitchen, I take a deep breath, scenting my pack and my mate. This is it. This is the moment I'm going to meet my mate for the first time. *Go slow Jackson, don't scare her away.* I say to myself.

Knowing there are people here and there is no way I'll walk in on my brother and his mate naked, I walk in without knocking. No one realizes I'm here at first, all busy talking and laughing as Remington and Jameson prepare food and the girls chat at the bar.

There she is. Mate. My cock hardens against my leg as we take her in for the first time. Her skin is pale, covered in a smattering of freckles, and looks soft to the touch. My hands itch with the need to run my fingers against her skin. Her strawberry blonde hair is loose, tucked behind her ears that have three tiny diamond earrings going up each ear. Fuck, she's sexy without even trying. She doesn't have on a stitch of makeup or any other jewelry and is dressed simply, in a white tank top that strains against her full tits.

"You made it!" Lillian shouts jumping off her barstool and running up to me to give me a big hug.

My mate looks up, her striking blue eyes taking me in, studying me curiously. Her plump pink lips rub together before she takes a sip of white wine, all the while staring at me. I hug my sister-in-law but release her quickly out of respect to my brother and more importantly my mate. While touch between pack members is part of pack life, something that brings us closer together, the only person I want touching me right now is my mate. More than want, I need her touch.

"Bout time you fucking showed up." Remington booms from across the kitchen, where he leans his ass against the island. There's a wicked look in his eyes and I suspect he can read what's going down.

"Jackson, come and meet my best friend Hannah. I don't think y'all have ever met before." Lillian says, walking towards my mate. My Hannah.

Hannah stands from where she's sitting at the island and walks up to me sticking out her hand confidently. "Hey Jackson, I'm Hannah. We seem to keep missing each other at these things." She says, an innocent smile curving at her lips.

I grab her hand in mine, rubbing my thumb against

her skin, and don't let go as I get a better look at the woman who is going to be mine for the rest of my life. She has no idea what she's awakened inside me. She is all of five foot four, maybe five foot five, and barely comes up to my chin. Her tits are more than a handful as they press against her white tank, her waist dips in and curves out to her wide hips. The worn jeans she has on are skintight against her thick ass and thighs. And like a cherry on top of a fucking perfect sundae, her toes are painted red. I'm fucking salivating, like a beast ready to sink his teeth into a rare piece of meat.

I wet my tongue against my lips as I prepare to say my first words to her. "Mine," my bear growls through me. Shit, that's not what I meant to say.

Hannah's eyes fly to mine as she nervously pulls her hand out of mine. "Excuse me?"

Hudson and Weston walk into the kitchen to see what's going on while Remington laughs awkwardly from my side and claps his big hand on my shoulder squeezing it hard. "What my idiot cousin meant to say is ... 'It's nice to meet you, Hannah. I've heard a lot of good things.' Isn't that right cuz?" He says looking at me meaningfully.

"That's right," I say, shrugging out of his grasp. Remington rolls his eyes and goes back to looking between Hannah and I expectantly like the creeper he is. "Pretty sure I just need to eat something," I say and rub my stomach as everyone in my pack gives me a knowing look.

Hannah smiles but it doesn't reach her eyes. I've

already fucked this up. *What the fuck Jackson, get your shit together.*

"Sooo, what's on the menu tonight? Anything I can help with?" I ask hoping to redirect the conversation.

"Oh shoot, I forgot the food in the car when I came in here to tell you about the bear!" Hannah announces then turns to walk out the door I just came in.

I follow her and when she goes to shut the door behind her, she hits my stomach instead. Hannah looks back at me and ends up tripping out the door, but before she falls, I grab her hand, steadying her.

"What are you doing?" She asks, quirking her brow.

"Giving you a hand," I say winking at her and kissing the top of her hand.

She blushes, it's hard to see in the dim light of the porch, but with my shifter senses, I catch it. She pulls her hand out of mine and starts walking to her car.

"So, what happened with the bear?"

Hannah looks over at me, her eyes big and round with excitement. "I was coming up the main road and about to turn down Jameson's driveway when a bear walked across the road and just stops and stares at me. I had to slam on my breaks so I wouldn't hit it. It was the weirdest thing."

"Good thing you didn't hit him."

"I know, right? At first, I was scared it was going to hurt me, but it didn't seem like it wanted to. It just ran off into the woods. It all happened so fast. I was in shock. I've never seen a bear before in real life." She finishes, stopping next to her car.

"Keep your eyes peeled, there's a family of them living out here in these woods."

"Really?" She asks, her eyes sparkling under the starlit sky.

I nod. "They don't hurt anyone. I'm pretty sure they just want to be left alone to live peacefully."

"It's so sad." She says before opening up her passenger side door and reaching down, sticking her sexy ass out, unknowingly giving me a great view.

"What is?" I ask clearing my throat.

Hannah pops back up, holding two glass containers that I take from her. "That hunters shoot bears just to take them home and mount them on the wall. What monster can do something like that?"

"I agree," I say then lift the dishes up to my nose and inhale. "Damn, Hannah. Whatever this is it smells heavenly."

"Chocolate trifle and corn casserole." She says proudly.

"I can't wait to get a taste." I groan, watching her ass sway in the moonlight as I follow her back into the house.

CHAPTER 4

After Jackson and I bring the food in from my car, all the guys go outside to start the bonfire. I don't miss the look Jackson gives me before he follows the guys out there.

Lillian and I stay in the kitchen to finish up dinner. "What do you think about Jackson?" She asks while stirring the potato salad.

"What do you mean?"

"He's cute right?"

She never asked what I thought about Rem, Huds, or Weston so I'm curious as to why she's pushing me on Jackson. Maybe my attraction to him is transparent to everyone. God, I hope not, that would be embarrassing. I want to tell her that the man who has to be a good foot taller than me is more than cute, but I refrain. He's her brother-in-law. I can't go there with him even if I want to desperately. "Sure."

Lillian rolls her eyes at me. "So, you don't feel anything towards him?" She presses.

"Lil, I just met the guy. What do you want me to do, tell you I love him?"

She shrugs with a lovesick look on her face. "Stranger things have happened," She says staring out the window at her husband who's talking with the rest of the guys. Jameson and Lillian fell in love instantly. The way she tells it, she knew immediately he was the one for her. Looking at them, you'd expect they've been together for a lifetime. I hope to find something close to what they have one day, but realistically I know relationships like theirs rarely happen.

I follow her gaze and my heart swells watching Jackson and Jameson work together to light the bonfire, Hudson and Remington goofing off, and Weston standing to the side silently overseeing everything. The Walker men are great men who work hard day in and day out for their family. No, they aren't perfect, but their hearts are good. Lillian has brought me into this family, a family like I've never known before.

"So, this lady comes running out of the woods naked, screaming 'You have to save me, there's a bear chasing me.' Hudson and I draw our dart guns as this big black furry thing come charging at us. At this point, we realize this isn't a real bear, but a Furry dressed like one."

"Wait, what's a Furry?" Lillian asks.

Remington looks at Jameson then Jameson whispers something in Lillian's ear and her face turns red. With big round eyes, she goes "oooh."

We all burst into laughter and she sticks her tongue out at us.

"So, we have the dart guns trained on this guy and we're ready to shoot him on principle or at least make him think we are. Who the hell dresses like a bear out in the woods? Then the lady comes back when she sees what we're about to do and starts pulling on Hudson's arm. Hudson ends up firing the dart gun and it hits the schmuck in the leg."

"Oh my god, what happened?" I ask, hanging onto their every word.

"Within seconds the guy goes limp and the woman starts beating the shit out of me for 'killing her husband,'" Hudson says rolling his eyes.

"It's not your fault he was dressed like a freaking bear running through the woods!"

"That's what I told her! She wasn't listening to anyone

though. She thought I actually shot him and was freaking out."

"So, what did you do?" Lillian asks.

"I pick him up and carry him over my shoulder to the next ranger station where we can call for an ambulance. The entire time she's bitching at Rem and me about calling the police and pressing charges."

"What an idiot," I say in outrage.

Hudson tips his beer at me. "You got it, sister."

"You think that's bad, wait 'til you hear about this patient I had back in North Dakota." Jameson starts. We all settle in listening to his story and about halfway through it hits me. I haven't been this happy, ever. It's been yet another great night with Lillian and her family. We've been sitting outside around the bonfire telling crazy stories about the people we have to deal with at our jobs. I look around the bonfire staring at the people who have given me more in the last few months than I've gotten from my family in the last ten years.

The twins are identical, but their personalities are night and day. Remington is the loud and obnoxious yet lovable one, while Hudson is the more reserved one of the two who also has a wicked sense of humor. Their older brother Weston looks somber all the time and it makes me want to give him a big hug whenever I see him. I should leave it alone since it isn't any of my business, but I need to find out from Lillian what's going on with him. These people feel like family, and family helps each other through the hard times.

I love coming to visit Lillian and her family. I feel free whenever I'm here. There's something about being able to come and be yourself, not having to worry about what people might think about you. I've always felt this way every time I come out to the Walker property. More than anything I feel like I belong here, and that's a feeling I haven't had since before my dad left me and my mom. Every time I have to leave, it gets harder and harder to go. It's crazy to feel this way about a group of people, but I guess that's what happens when you find your tribe. Damn, I found my people.

"What are you smiling about?" Jackson leans over and asks me quietly.

I shake my head at him, not wanting to tell him my thoughts. Over the last couple of hours, I've learned more about the Walker family. Weston works from home and I already knew Jameson since he's a doctor at the hospital I work at. We often worked the same schedule before Lillian's accident. Since then he only works the day shift. Jackson, the sexy police lieutenant, works at the police station and seems to love it going by what he's said tonight. All of the Walker men are tall, muscular, attractive men, but there's something different about Jackson.

Jackson gives me a knowing smile and rests a warm hand over my knee and my heart skips a beat in my chest.

"Are you okay?" He asks rubbing his thumb against my knee and looking concerned.

I nod and stand quickly. "Who is ready for dessert?"

Everyone shouts 'me' and 'I am', making me laugh as I walk away from the bonfire. Those guys can really put away some food. After everything they ate tonight, they shouldn't be able to eat dessert.

I had to get away from Jackson for a few minutes. He was making me feel things I've never felt before, want things I never thought I could have. Men like him don't fall for broken girls like me. I need to keep my distance so I don't get my heart broken and can keep this new family I have.

I pull the chocolate trifle out of the fridge and put it on the counter. When I take the lid off, I lean over to smell it and end up getting chocolate on my shirt. "Damnit." I groan.

I pull the tank top I have on over my head and start rinsing it off in the sink, not wanting it to stain. Someone walks in the back door and my heart sputters, not wanting to be caught without my tank top on. I'm wearing a bra and a white camisole, so it's not like I'm naked, but the camisole doesn't do a very good job of concealing much.

"God damn, baby." Jackson groans a few feet away from me.

I look over at him and freeze, not knowing what to do. He inches closer until he's pressing me against the counter, his hand reaching behind me to turn off the water.

"You have a little bit of chocolate right here," He says in a guttural tone, swiping a smear of chocolate from the top of my breast with his index finger. I watch as he sticks his finger in his mouth and moans as he licks it clean. "I fucking love chocolate." He says before taking my mouth in a demanding kiss.

His kiss lights the match and I'm instantly engulfed with need. Jackson wraps his arms around my back and pulls me away from the sink just enough so that he can pick me up, hands under my ass, and sit me down on the counter in front of him. Standing between my spread thighs, he presses his body against mine, his hard cock pressing against my throbbing core while he devours my mouth. His tongue takes what I willingly give as one of his hands slides into my hair, clutching onto the strands as he pulls my neck to the side and kisses down my throat to my breasts. His other hand slips under my camisole and rubs against my back.

"Hey Hannah, what's the hold up with the... oh!" Remington asks, barging into the kitchen.

Embarrassed, I lean my forehead against Jackson's shoulder not wanting Remington to see me like this. "Get the fuck out Rem," Jackson growls.

"Yeah, yeah. I'm going fucker." He mumbles walking out of the kitchen and back outside.

When I hear the door close, I look up and see Jackson staring down at me. I look away biting my swollen bottom lip. "Easy there love. Don't go hiding on me now." Jackson says, holding my face in the palms of his hands.

"I'm not this girl, Jackson. I don't make out with men I just met. I certainly don't do what we just did."

"I sure as hell hope not." He laughs, the sound sending a shiver down my back.

Reaching up with my right hand I cover his, looking at him. "We shouldn't have done this."

"Why the fuck not?" He asks, his smile quickly fading. He steps out of my reach and paces in front of me. "We are two consenting adults Hannah, we did nothing wrong."

"But Lillian-" I try.

"Lillian would understand better than anyone!" He says, cutting me off.

I slide off the counter to grab my hoodie off the kitchen island and pull it over my head. When I grab my purse and shove my tank top into it, Jackson stands in front of me, arms crossed over his chest. "What are you doing?"

"I think it's time for me to go."

"Hannah don't go. Not because of what we just shared, that should be the reason you're staying, not leaving."

"I'm not willing to lose Lillian because of whatever this is between us. It's not worth it."

Jackson stumbles back as if my words physically struck him. He stares at me, studying my face for a long time until he finally sighs and drops his chin. "I'm not going to stop you tonight, but there is going to come a time real soon when leaving is the last thing you'll want to do and when that time comes, I'm going to hold on tight and never let you leave. Until then, I'm going to prove to you how 'worth it' what we have really is."

I doubt it, love like that doesn't exist, at least not for me. Jackson is a good man, one that is commanding and exudes confidence like I've never seen before. If I were to make a list of traits my perfect man would have, Jackson has them all, and I pushed him away knowing this.

I nod and Jackson steps out of my way. Walking away from him feels wrong, but I do it, believing it's what is best. I walk out of the back door and to the bonfire where everyone looks at me smiling. Obviously, Remington told everyone what he walked in on. When Lillian spots my purse, her brows pull together. "You're leaving?"

I shrug. "It's getting late," I say, offering the lamest excuse in the world.

"Here, I'll walk with you to your car."

"No, don't get up. It's just right there." I say gesturing with my head towards my car. She's sitting in Jameson's lap and looks comfortable.

"Psshh." Lillian stands and loops her arm through mine.

I wave goodnight to the rest of the guys and walk with Lillian back to my car.

When we're far enough way Lillian nudges me. "What happened?" She whispers.

"Nothing." I sigh.

"That's not what Rem said." She jokes.

"Rem has a big mouth and needs to learn to keep it shut." I laugh.

"I heard that!" He shouts from the bonfire making everyone burst into a fit of laughter. When I look back to glare at him, Jackson is standing beside Jameson, his eyes on me, no trace of a smile on his face. Shit, I really pissed off the big guy.

"How could he hear that?" I say out loud.

"They have really good hearing. Like freakishly good."

I nod as if that explains the superhero hearing he just displayed.

When I open my car door, I roll the window down to talk to Lillian before I go. She leans down on the door through the open window to look at me. "Jackson is a good man Hannah."

"I know he is."

"Then what's the problem?"

"Guys always seem perfect at the beginning of a relationship Lil. Then you get to know them, and something eventually changes. They aren't the Prince Charming you thought they once were. Maybe you don't even realize anything has changed until they come to you one day and tell you that you aren't what they want anymore. What happens when that happens with Jackson and me? What happens when he has another woman around? Being around all of you won't be the same. It will hurt and then I won't only have lost Jackson, I'll have lost all of you. I'm not willing to risk that."

"That won't happen, not with Jackson."

I shake my head. "There's no way you can know that."

Lillian is about to say something, but she stops and gives me a sad look. There's something she isn't telling me, but I need to go before Jackson walks over here and all the walls I'm putting up between us fall back down with all of his charm.

I crank the engine and Lillian backs away so I can leave. Well, I try to crank the engine, but nothing happens. I try again but all I hear are small ticking noises. My car has plenty of gas and I just took it in for an oil change a few weeks ago, what the hell is going on? I try cranking the engine again and again, but it never turns over. I bang my head against the wheel and groan.

"What's the problem Hannah Banana? Forget to fill up before you came out here?" I hear Remington ask from beside me.

When I look up, I see that Jackson is standing beside Rem, arms crossed over his chest and brows pulled together. All of the guys are standing around my car. "Ha ha ha. I have gas you jerk."

"Pop the hood," Weston says standing in front of my car, Hudson ready with a small flashlight turned on and shining at the hood.

It takes me a minute to find the lever, but I do and pull it. Jackson opens my door and reaches his hand out to me. "Let me get in there and have a look around."

I take his hand and he helps me out of my car then

kisses me on the cheek before sliding the seat as far back as it will go and sits down where I just was.

Lillian and I stand and watch all five of the guys talk and troubleshoot. Jameson joins Weston and Hudson at the front of my car with another flashlight. Remington stands next to Jackson, asking him question after question.

"Do you think it's-"

Jackson shakes his head. "Already tried that. Rem, I love you man, but shut the hell up and let me think."

After about twenty minutes of the guys messing around under the hood of my car, Weston slams it shut and walks up to me.

"I can't find anything wrong with it. Was it driving funny earlier?"

I try thinking back but nothing stands out. "Not really. I mean it seemed a little slower than usual today, but it's an older car, I figured that was why."

CHAPTER 5

JACKSON

Someone messed with her fucking car. That's the only answer I can come up with and I'm betting it's the asshole I scented on her car earlier. I look over at Weston and he gives me a knowing look. They probably scented someone all over her engine. I tap my nose nonchalantly and he gives me a curt nod. Fuck.

"Hannah, I'll give you a ride home. Come on honey." I say, nodding toward my truck.

"But what about my car?" She asks with a catch in her voice.

Shit. The last thing I want is for her to start crying. My bear won't be able to deal with that, he'll need to comfort her. I nod my head over at Weston. "The engine master and I will take a look at her tomorrow and hopefully get her running for you."

"You're a mechanic?" She asks looking at Weston.

"I dabble."

"He doesn't give himself enough credit. The man could rebuild an engine in his sleep." Hudson says slapping Weston on the back.

Hannah smiles. "You're just an everyday man's man, aren't you? What else can you do?"

He shrugs and says nothing. The guy keeps himself busy so that he has no time to think about what he's lost.

Sighing, Hannah's shoulders drop. "Thank you, Weston, for looking at my car, and Jackson, I'll take that ride if you don't mind."

"Mind? It would be my pleasure. And Hannah, you don't ever have to thank us. We take care of those in our pack." I say without thinking and opening the passenger door of my truck.

"Pack?" She asks quirking her head to the side.

"Crew, group, family." Hudson lists off effortlessly with an easy smile. "You're part of ours now Hannah."

When Hannah smiles at him a small part of me gets jealous. I want all of her smiles. Every single one. It's not sane how I feel, but it is what it is. If I have to share her smiles with my pack I will, doesn't mean I'm going to like it.

"Text me when you get home," Lillian says giving Hannah a hug then she steps back into Jameson's embrace.

"Ready?" Hannah asks.

When I give her a nod, she reaches up and grabs the 'oh shit' handle in my truck and swings her ass into the seat. I close her door then run around to the driver's side of my truck and get in. My pack stands and watches me as I pull out of the driveway.

Our drive is quiet except for the country music playing in the background while I drive her home. She gives me directions when needed, but other than that she says nothing.

"It's the blue house on the right." She says pointing to a small bungalow style home.

I pull into her driveway and look around. There are no streetlights close to her home and her house is completely dark. If anyone messed with her car, no one would have been able to see.

"Give me your phone for a minute," I say reaching out my hand to her.

"Why?" She asks, placing it in my hand.

I quickly shoot off a text message to my phone then add myself as a contact. "I'm putting my number in here that way if you need anything you can call me."

I hand her back the phone and she drops it into her purse then grabs the door handle. I'm waiting for her to get out, but she pauses.

"What is it?" I ask watching her chew her bottom lip thinking through what she wants to say.

"This doesn't change anything from earlier. I'm sorry about the kiss, but I'm not going to hook up randomly with my best friend's brother-in-law."

It changes everything, but I'm not going to argue with

her. She's my mate and there isn't anyone else in the universe who will ever make me feel the way she does. She's the one woman made for me, to not only be my wife, but my partner, and my best friend. She's human and doesn't understand, so I'll slow things down and do things the human way if that's what she needs. One thing I'll never do is let her go, not ever.

"Who said anything about a random hookup?"

She fidgets with the strap of her bag. "You know what I mean Jackson."

I grab one of her hands in mine and wait to speak until she's looking at me. "How about we take this slow, be friends, and see where things go? No pressure."

"You don't understand!" She growls and pulls her hand out of mine, sounding just like a pissed off female bear.

"Explain it to me then," I shout, frustrated she won't give us a chance.

"If we hooked up things would be weird after, even if we promise they won't be. And, I'm not that girl. I don't do things with men with no feelings involved. I'll get attached, what happens then?"

I'm about to respond when she interrupts me.

"I'll tell you what happens. We date then eventually break things off and Lillian is put in this uncomfortable position, being forced to take her family's side or mine."

"That's one hell of an assumption."

"It's inevitable. It might not happen exactly like that, but the end will be the same. I'm not risking my friendship with Lillian or your family for something that is doomed from the beginning." Hannah says, shaking her head. Without letting me get a word in, she gets out of my truck and walks up the pathway to her front door.

Sighing, I follow behind her and stand silently with her as she searches her purse for her keys to unlock the door.

Where did she get all of these negative ideas about relationships from? I remind myself that I know what we are, but she has no idea. Telling her that we're fated mates, meant to be together forever won't be enough. I want her to love me for me, not because I told her she is my mate. This is going to make things harder, but anything worth having is worth every ounce of struggle. I won't ever give up on her, no matter how long it takes her to feel the same way I already feel. For me, I loved her in an instant. I know with everything inside me she's mine and I'll always love her. Either she's fighting our bond hard or the walls she has guarding her heart are made of steel and our bond can't penetrate them.

"It's pretty dark out here. You should leave the light on near your door."

"I usually do, but the light bulb went out a few weeks ago. I've been meaning to change it, but I keep forgetting."

A few weeks ago? I want to grab her by the shoulders and shake some sense into her. I try and tramp down all of the frustration I'm feeling, knowing it won't do us any good for me to go off half-cocked. Her safety is of the utmost importance to me. I've lived through the war and have seen too many people killed senselessly. When she unlocks her door, I step in ahead of her and fumble around for a light switch.

"Jackson, what are you doing?" She asks flipping a switch and lighting up the room.

"Always with the questions," I mumble walking through her simple but tidy living room.

Hannah stops short in the middle of her living room and folds her arms over her chest, watching me curiously while I make a sweep of her combined kitchen and dining room.

When I'm satisfied no one is in the main area of her home, I stop a few feet from her. The mating bond is pushing me to do more, but it doesn't seem that Hannah is feeling what I am. After how Lillian reacted to Jameson, I had hoped our mating bond would be just as strong. "Look Hannah, you don't have a security system, you have a flimsy lock on your door, and your lights have been out for hours. I'm checking to make sure your place is secure before I leave you."

"What would make you believe it isn't?" She asks, her brows pulling together.

"Besides everything I just listed?" I ask in frustration, running my hands through my hair. She gives me an irritated look and I sigh. "I don't like that your car is all of a sudden giving you trouble. It could be nothing, old age like you said, but it could also be that someone messed with it."

"Shit, I didn't even think of that. But why would… do you really think someone messed with my car?" She asks, staring at me with suddenly wide eyes. There's something she's holding back, and that worries me more than anything.

I walk up to her and rub her upper arms, trying to calm her down. "It's a possibility I don't want to rule out. Let me look around inside your place and make sure it's safe for you. I won't be able to sleep tonight if I don't."

"Okay." She relents.

I check all three bedrooms and two bathrooms then make another sweep around the living area. Satisfied that no one has been in here, scenting no one but Hannah, I walk back to where Hannah has been standing since I left her.

She's looking a little more tired than rattled at this point though. "Find anything?" I shake my head no and she lets out an audible sigh. "Good." She says sounding relieved.

I walk to the front door with Hannah following close behind me. She reaches for the door and I grab her hand, placing a kiss on top. "If you want me to stay the night to keep an eye on things just say the word."

After thinking about it for a moment she shakes her head. "I'll be alright Jackson. I've been on my own for the last few years. I can take care of myself."

"I'm going to get going. I'll call you tomorrow to let you know what we find out about your car." It kills me that she doesn't need me as I need her. "Call me if you need anything, no matter what time it is. I'll be here. Okay?" I say staring down into her bright blue eyes.

"I will." She says and opens the door for me to leave.

"I'll see you tomorrow Hannah."

She opens her mouth, but then closes it and shakes her head. "See you tomorrow Jackson."

I can swear she wants to say more, but she doesn't as she shuts the door behind me. Once she locks it, I walk back to my truck and sit there a while watching the house. After a few minutes, a text comes through on my phone.

Hannah: *What are you doing?*
    Me: *See there you go again with all those questions*

She sends me an eye roll emoji and I laugh out loud in the silence of my dark truck.

Hannah: *No really, why haven't you left yet?*

• • •

I look up at her house and see the curtains shift closed and a dark shadow behind them.

M*e: Are you checking me out from your bedroom window?*

T hree dots pop up in the chat then disappear. They pop up a couple of times before she finally texts back.

H*annah: Not right now.*
Me: Good to know.
Hannah: Don't you have to get home for work tomorrow?
Me: No. I'm off. What about you? Will you need a ride to work?
Hannah: No, I'm off too.

I think to ask her if I can take her to a movie or out for dinner, but I don't. I need to take this slow no matter how much it kills me and my bear to do so. I take one final look at the house checking to see if anything stands out that's out of the ordinary. Is there anything that shouldn't be there? Not that I can tell, everything looks normal, but I could have missed something. I didn't notice anyone's scent other than Hannah's though, so that makes me feel marginally better.

M*e: Goodnight sweet Hannah*
Hannah: Goodnight <3

I walk into Weston's garage where he is elbow deep in Hannah's car. "What do you think?" I ask.

He looks up and I toss him a rag when I see the amount of grease covering his forearms and hands.

"Thanks, man." He says wiping as much grease off as he can.

Nodding, I take a sip from my water bottle and wait for him to tell me what he knows.

Weston leans against the side of her car and crosses his arms over his chest staring at me. "Pretty sure someone put something in her gas tank."

I throw the water bottle across the garage. "That mother fucker! When I find out who did this, I'm going to tear him apart!" I roar.

Weston steps up to me and squeezes my shoulders. "And we'll be right there with you Jacks, but you need to cool it. You do this shit for a living, use your head and find the guy. Right now, we need to finish flushing the tank to get this piece-of-shit car up and running again for your mate."

"Does everyone know?" I grin, liking the sound of that. *Mate.*

Weston doesn't say anything, but his look tells me everything I need to know. Of course, they know. I've never acted that way with another woman and neither have they, except Jameson.

We spend the rest of the afternoon working on Hannah's car. After flushing the fuel tank, we topped her fluids and filled her tires with air. While tinkering around under the hood, Weston found a few parts that needed replacing and put the order in. He said it would be a few days before they came in. She needs a new car badly, her Camry is on its last leg, but this gives me the perfect opportunity to spend time with my mate.

CHAPTER 6

HANNAH

I've been keeping myself busy today by cleaning my small house from top to bottom and folding the piles of clean laundry I've let build up. I've picked up my phone what feels like a hundred times to check it and see if I've missed a call or text from him, but I haven't. I've even typed out a text to Jackson a few times but deleted them all, convincing myself I'm being foolish. Really, I'm just nervous as hell to talk to him again after the kiss we shared.

Ever since Jackson walked out of my house last night, I've wanted to call him and tell him to come back. More than wanted to, I've felt compelled to. It's as if my body needs him close. As crazy as it sounds, I feel like he took a part of me with him when he left. I haven't felt right all day and with every hour that passes, I'm going crazy thinking about him, needing him here.

The kiss we shared last night was hot as hell and something I've replayed over and over deep into the night, and all day today. I had never kissed a man before Jackson. Sure, there were a couple of boys in high school, but it never went past a kiss. While I was curious about sex and physical attraction, the kisses always felt wrong, the boys never seemed right, and I never wanted anything more. Everything changed last night. I didn't just want more from Jackson, I wanted everything from him.

What is it about him that is so different than any other man I've met before? Sure, there have been men I've thought were attractive, but none that I ever considered a relationship with. In the years since my father left my mother and me, I've kept my distance from men, not wanting to feel the same heartbreak my mother did. Loneliness seemed like a better option than having to go through the pain of losing someone later on.

With Jackson, there's nothing worse than denying what we could be. All of the bullshit I spouted last night about us never working out was exactly that. The truth is I'm scared. Scared that he is just like the man who shaped my view of what men are like and how they treat their partners. I didn't believe what I said, but I said it, pushing him away thinking I was doing what was best. If I gave into him, he could be the man I never dreamed existed, but he could also be the man that sets my world on fire and not in a sexy way. My head keeps telling me everything that could go wrong, everything I could lose, but my heart and my body won't listen. I want Jackson Walker with a fierceness I've never known before.

Tired of holding myself back, I pick up my phone to call him. Before I can find him in my contacts, his name pops up and it's him who is calling me. A big smile covers my face.

"Hello," I answer, staring out the large windows in my living room watching my neighbor walk her dog along the sidewalk.

"You sound happy today." His rough yet gentle voice says.

"I was hoping you had good news about my car."

"Damn girl, way to break my heart. Here I was thinking you were happy to hear from me."

A stupid grin stretches across my face, making my cheeks burn. "Maybe." I giggle. Who am I right now? I clear my throat. "But really, how is my car?"

"The good news is Weston knows what's wrong with it."

"That is good. What's the bad news?"

"He had to order a few parts, so you'll be without your vehicle until it's fixed. Once the parts are in, he'll get your car up and running. He said it could take up to a week to get your car back to you though."

"How much is that going to run?" I worry aloud, already knowing I don't have much in savings to pay for this.

"We've got you. Don't worry about the cost."

Of course, he says that. I'll have to think of another way to pay Weston back for fixing my car. Relieved I will have a working vehicle soon, now I need to figure out how I will get to work for the next week. The downside to living in Berkley Springs is that it isn't big enough to have a bus line or even Uber drivers. I'll have to text one of the girls from my shift and see if they mind picking me up and taking me home. I'm sure Lori wouldn't mind, she's always been a sweetheart. I take a deep breath, happy with the plan I have in place, sort of.

"I'll be taking you to work and bringing you home until your car is fixed."

"You don't have to do that. I'm sure I can get one of the girls from work to give me a ride."

"I'd prefer it. Look there's something else we need to discuss."

"What?"

"We think someone put something in your gas tank. That's why it wouldn't start."

I fall to my couch as what he said sinks in. "So, someone did mess with my car. When you suggested it last night, I didn't think it was a possibility. Why would someone do that?" I question, mentally running through the people I know.

"No idea. Have you pissed anyone off lately?"

"I literally go to work and hang out with Lillian. There's no one I can think of that I don't get along with."

"Most of the time it's someone you don't suspect. I'll

drive you to and from work which will give me a chance to check out the people you're around on a daily basis."

"I work the night shift. It will be easier to get one of my friends

from work to give me a ride."

"What if it's one of your friends?"

"I doubt that."

"Please let me do this Hannah. It will give me peace of mind knowing you are getting to and from work safely."

There really isn't any reason not to let him drive me and he does have a point. "Okay, I need to be at the hospital at seven tomorrow night."

"That's not a problem." An awkward silence hangs in the air. Before he called, all I wanted was to talk to him and see where this thing between us could go, but now I want to hole up in my bed and escape this sudden new reality. Whoever put something in my gas tank, were they trying to hurt me? And if so, why?

"Please don't worry about this. I'll find out who messed with your car and they'll answer for what they've done."

"Thanks," I offer flatly. "I'll see you tomorrow," I say and hang up, not bothering to hear anything else he has to say. For the first time since I moved to Berkley Springs over seven years ago, I feel unsafe.

My phone chimes and I pick it up to see I have a text from Jackson.

Jackson: What are you doing right now?

I look at the time on my phone and see that it's a little after five. I'm getting in a few more minutes of sleep before I get ready for work. This morning I woke up at nine o'clock, having had the worst night's rest I've ever had. Needless to say, I've been in a shitty mood all day. I laid down an hour ago hoping to get a nap in, instead I laid awake thinking about everything weighing on my mind.

Me: Not a lot. About to start getting ready for work.
          Jackson: I was thinking about bringing dinner over before I took you in. Have you eaten yet?

I think to tell him not to bother, but I haven't felt like eating all day and my stomach chooses now to rumble.

·   ·   ·

Me: *That sounds great.*

Jackson: What are your thoughts on Chinese takeout?

Me: Yum!

Jackson: (Laughing emoji) I'll take that as a yes. Anything you want specifically?

Me: LOL. Pork fried rice is my favorite.

Jackson: You got it. See you in about thirty minutes.

Thirty minutes? Shit! I roll out of bed and run to the bathroom to jump in the shower. I'm in and out in less than ten minutes, taking a faster shower than I normally do. I put on some eyeshadow, a few strokes of mascara, and some lip gloss. Pleased with my look, I twirl my long hair into a bun and change into my dark blue scrub pants, leaving my top off until right before work. I have on a white long sleeve shirt so I won't get cold in the ER tonight. I spray a few squirts of my favorite Bath and Body Works body spray, Wild Madagascar Vanilla all over me.

I walk out to my living room and quickly straighten up, folding a throw blanket and organizing the things on my coffee table. Checking my watch, I see Jackson will be showing up any minute now. Looking at my small kitchen table I regret not tackling it today. It's more of a dumping ground for mail and things that need to be put away than a place to eat. It's been years since I've eaten there. Usually, I'll eat in the living room on my couch. I consider cleaning it off and grabbing the unused placemats out of the drawer but before I can decide there's a knock at the door.

My heart threatens to beat out of my chest as I walk to my door and open it.

"Hello beautiful." Jackson grins, his double dimples popping out and making me swoon. He's standing there looking sexy as hell in his black Berkley Springs Police Department uniform that hugs his body perfectly. The fact that he's holding a bag of Chinese takeout only adds to his sexiness.

"Can I come in? Or are you going to stand there and stare at me for a few more minutes?" He says and winks.

My cheeks burn with embarrassment, but I don't let that stop me from opening the door wider and inviting him in. I mean he is holding the goods.

Jackson walks in and goes straight to my kitchen where he immediately starts pulling white food containers out of the brown bag he was carrying. I grab two plates out of the cabinet and two forks out of the drawer and set them down on the counter.

"Jeeze Louise Jackson, it's just the two of us!" I exclaim looking at all of the containers he's placed on the counter.

"I wasn't sure what you wanted, all you told me was pork fried rice. I got some chicken and broccoli, kung pao chicken, dumplings, crab rangoons, pork lo mein, white rice, and your pork fried rice."

"Who is going to eat all of this?" I laugh.

Jackson, who is looking adorably confused and his brows drawn together says, "we are."

"Okay, there big guy. Let's get into it then, we need to leave in about forty-five minutes to get me to work on time."

Handing Jackson a plate and fork we proceed to fill our plates with delicious looking food. My mouth is watering just smelling all of it. Walking into the living room, I put my plate down on the table and go back to the kitchen to grab two bottles of water. Coming back, I hand Jackson his bottle and settle in beside him, criss crossing my legs.

"This is so good," I say after swallowing my first bite. "Did you get this at The Noodle House?"

Jackson shakes his head while swallowing his food. "There's this hole in the wall place next to the police station I always go to. You wouldn't know it by looking at the place, but they make the best food."

"Yeah, they do. This is seriously the best pork fried rice I've ever had."

Jackson finishes before I do and goes to get a second plate which he finishes before I finish my first.

"I have no idea how you guys eat so much. Like where do you put it?"

Jackson laughs. "We burn a lot of energy."

"Apparently so."

"How long have you lived here?"

I look around my house and smile sadly. "Since I was in high school. It was my grandma's house. She left it to me when she passed away."

"Where are your parents?" He asks.

"Dad is back in Chicago, where I'm from. Last time I heard from Mom she was in some tiny town I've never heard of in South America."

"Any brothers or sisters?"

"The woman my father left my mother for has a few kids and they had a couple together. I'm not really close with them though."

"That has to be hard."

I shrug not wanting to talk about them. "It is what it is. What about you? Is Jameson your only brother?"

"Yeah. Mom and Dad stopped after me. Rem, Huds, and Wes are as close as brothers though. Moving away from our family brought us closer together."

"What made you all move here from... I'm sorry I know I've been told this before, but I can remember where you're from."

"Small town in North Dakota. All of our family are there. It was a great place to grow up, but we all got to the point where we knew we needed to leave to find our future."

I want to ask him if he's found what he's looking for but decide against it. That's liable to open up a can of worms I'm not ready for.

"How does my car look otherwise?"

Jackson winces. "Camrys are good cars, but after so many miles, wear and tear take its toll, even on the best machine. You need to start thinking about letting it go and getting something more reliable."

"I was worried you were going to say that." I sigh as my stomach sinks a little and the thought of stretching my budget to include a car payment becomes a near reality.

"Hey, don't worry, Weston will keep it running as long as you need it to."

My phone chimes, alerting me that I need to get going so I'm not late for work. "Shoot." I murmur.

"Time to go?" Jackson asks.

I smile and nod.

"Here. Let me take that. I'll put the rest of the food away. You go do what you need to do."

"Thank you," I tell him and rush to my room to finish getting ready. I pull my scrub top on, spray on a little bit more of my body spray, touch up my lip gloss and pull my tennis shoes on.

When I walk back out to the living room Jackson is leaning against the arm of the couch, arms folded across his chest, staring down at his feet. As soon as he hears me walk in, he looks up and his warm, golden brown eyes hold me captive. I suck in a sharp breath, unprepared for the look he's leveling me with.

"Come here."

Slowly I walk towards him. When I get close, he snags

me by the wrist and pulls me in between his legs, his hands settling on my hips. His hands are gripping me tightly, but not so much that it hurts. The heat that's pulsing between us is intoxicating.

"I'm going to kiss you now." He says.

"Okay," I gasp, and he captures my lips with his own.

CHAPTER 7

HANNAH

It's been three days. Three days and I can't stop smiling, and thinking, and dreaming about that damn kiss. The kiss that changed something inside me. And that was just one of many.

Every night he brings dinner over and before I have a chance to finish getting ready, he has me pressed against a wall, the counter, or the couch. Any surface really that traps me to him. I'm not complaining. While we've spent a lot of time kissing, we've also spent as much time learning one another. What I've learned, I like, more than like, but I'm not saying that word yet.

I'm so caught up in my thoughts of Jackson I don't hear someone walk into the patient's room I'm in. His arm wraps around my waist and he leans in close, too close, to take a look at the chart I am supposed to be reading. His hot breath pants against my neck and as soon as I feel him, I jerk away, his touch feeling all wrong.

I turn and see that it's Dr. Hammond and I'm not in the least bit surprised. Disgusted that he touched me? Yes. Surprised? No. "Don't you ever put your hands on me again," I whisper shout.

His eyes dark eyes send a chill through me. "Come on Hannah, we will be good together." He says walking towards me with a creepy smile on his face.

I'm backing away from him, but unfortunately, he has me cornered. "No, we won't."

Dr. Hammond reaches me easily and grabs my wrists, holding them behind my back in one of his large hands. "No one tells me no." He barks.

"I just did," I say through clenched teeth.

I look down at the patient who is in a coma and unaware of what is about to happen. Dr. Hammond laughs coldly, running his free hand up and under my scrub top.

Fuck this. I raise my leg and drop it down as hard as I can, digging my foot into his. As soon as he releases me, I grab the remote and press the call button.

"Hello?" Lori asks.

I'm about to scream for help when Dr. Hammond slams his hand against my mouth holding it there as he pushes me against the wall. "You say anything to anyone I'll have you fired. It will be the word of a young nurse against that of a distinguished doctor. No one will hire you.

You won't be able to get a job anywhere. Keep your fucking mouth shut. Do you hear me?"

I nod my head up and down quickly willing to agree to anything to get him away from me.

"Is everything okay in here?" Lori asks from the door.

Dr. Hammond drops his hand immediately and moves away from me. The room is dark, and I don't know how much she can see, but I assume it isn't a lot. "Hannah had a question and luckily I was walking by just as she was calling. You should know better than to use the call button, Hannah. Please stop by my office at the end of your shift so we can discuss the protocol in these situations."

"Yyyes Dr. Hammond." I stutter.

He nods and walks out of the room.

Lori stares at me for a long time then turns to leave.

"That's not what happened," I tell her.

She gives me a sad look. "I know." She says and walks out of the room.

She knows? What the fuck? Did this happen to her too? I put the chart back where it goes and rush to the bathroom on the verge of being sick and lock the door. I'm so fucking pissed. How dare he put his hands on me. How dare he talk to me like that. No one gets to talk to me and treat me that way. Angry hot tears stream down my face. I don't know if I've ever been this angry before, not even after Dad left. How many women have stayed silent and let him get away with this over and over again? God, I'm so fucking pissed I could scream. It takes everything inside me to hold it together.

Eventually, I look up and catch my reflection in the mirror. I'm a hot mess. Black mascara is streaming down my red face. Jesus.

My phone vibrates in my pocket and I pull it out see Jackson has texted me, telling me he's on his way to pick me up. I don't know what I'm supposed to do. After cleaning my face up so that no one knows I'm upset, I make sure I've done everything I need to do before leaving. When I go to clock out Lori barely even looks at me. Really? I wasn't the one in there abusing my power and attacking a nurse, it was him. She can't even look at me.

My nerves are shot, and my anxiety is at an all-time high as I go to get my purse from my locker. I pass Dr. Hammond on my way out but keep walking not wanting to give him another opportunity.

Jackson is still in his truck when I pull the door handle and hop in swiftly.

"What's wrong?"

"Nothing, I'm just tired," I answer hoping he'll let it drop. He's still parked in front of the hospital when I see Dr. Hammond walk out to go to his car.

"Can we just leave?" I yell. He doesn't understand and it's not his fault, but my need to escape is the only thing I feel.

Jackson jerks back and I immediately regret what I said. He pulls his truck away from the curb and starts the quick drive back to my house. "Come on baby, tell me what's going on. What happened?" He says in a calm voice and tries holding my hand, but I shift away from him, leaning my head against the window. This is so fucking messed up.

"Can't I just have a bad day?" I ask when a tear falls down my cheek. I try wiping it away before he sees it, but I'm not quick enough.

Jackson pulls his truck over on the side of the road and unbuckles my seatbelt. He slides his seat back and looks at me. "Get over here." He demands in a tone I've never heard from him before.

I crawl over to him and as soon as my ass is in his lap I break down, crying into his shirt.

"Oh baby, tell me what's wrong." He soothes, rubbing my back.

After a minute I'm able to chill out and dry my face. How do I tell him about this? He's a cop and knowing him he'll go for blood. I don't even know if there's anything to press charges on.

Jackson curls his finger under my chin and lifts it so that I'm looking at him. When I see the tenderness in his eyes, I bit my lip to keep myself from crying more. "Whatever it is just tell me. We'll get through it together, okay?"

I nod and take a deep breath, blowing it out slowly. "It was the end of my shift. I was in a patient's room checking on them. I wasn't paying attention when a doctor put his arm around me and got close." Jackson's body stiffens, but he remains silent, holding me in his strong hands. "I immediately backed away and told him never to touch me again."

"Good, what did the fuckwad do?"

"He said we would be good together. When I told him no, it pissed him off and he pushed me against a wall and put my hands behind my back so I couldn't move. He started to put his hand up my shirt, that's when I stomped on his foot, pressed the call button, and tried getting away. But then he shoved me against the wall with his hand over my mouth and told me if I said anything, he'd get me fired."

I've never seen Jackson look as pissed as he does at this moment. I don't know what to do or say so I try sliding off of his lap to give him space, but he stops me.

"No, I need you here." He growls.

I know he's not pissed at me, so I stay. "Okay, I'm here," I say, trying to calm the beast inside him.

Jackson closes his eyes and leans his head on my shoulder. After a couple of minutes of silence, he takes a deep breath then looks up. "Let me get this straight. He fucking assaulted you then threatened you?"

"Yeah. I mean assaulted might be a strong-"

"Did he put his hands on you in a way you didn't like, without your consent, and cause you harm?"

"Yes." I say without needing to think about it.

"That's assault."

"Can I press charges?" I ask ready to nail this guy's balls to the wall.

"Absofuckinglutely," Jackson says with a proud grin on his face.

Instead of taking me home, Jackson takes me to the police station so I can file charges against Dr. Hammond. I give my statement and then write it down and sign it. It's still crazy to me that I'm the only person who has ever come forward against him. When Jackson dropped me off at home, he assured me Dr. Hammond would be arrested today and put in jail. Once I got home, I took a long hot shower and crawled into bed. I was worried it would take me awhile to fall asleep, but thankfully it didn't.

I woke up at a quarter to five and called out of work, knowing my head wouldn't be in the game today. I also called the human resources department at the hospital and reported the assault and that I had pressed charges against him. They were shocked and more than anything concerned that this had happened at their hospital. They apologized and told me his actions would not be tolerated.

***

JACKSON

The idea of wrapping my hands around the doctor's neck and squeezing the life out of him has crossed my mind several times. I've also contemplated shifting into my bear and eating him, but I'm not that depraved. The only thing holding me off is the fact that he's been in jail the past two nights.

Ever since Hannah came home Thursday morning, one of the members of my pack has been there, patrolling outside her home when I couldn't be. I've taken the night-shift the past two nights, shifting to my bear once I've left her house for the evening and keeping a watchful eye out. Thank god her street is almost pitch-black, or her neighbors might be freaking out if they saw a huge ass grizzly walking the perimeter of her house and sleeping under her window.

HANNAH

It's Saturday morning and today is the day I get my car back. Jackson let me know last night while he was over with dinner that Weston got all the parts in and should be finished with my car sometime today. I'm so excited to get it back and be free to go and do as I please.

Doctor Hammond was arrested Thursday afternoon and I couldn't be happier, although I worry about what's going to happen next.

There's a knock at my door. My heart skips a beat and I hope that on the other side of the door will be Jackson holding my keys. I open the door without checking the peephole and find the last person I expect to be standing on my doorstep.

"Dr. Hammond?" I ask startled. He's standing there in a crumpled red polo shirt and dark jeans. This is probably the most disheveled I've ever seen the arrogant piece of shit. What the hell does he think he's doing showing up to my home? More importantly, why isn't he in jail?

"Hannah, I've told you to call me Chris." He says stepping towards me. Instinctually I back away giving him the opening he needs to walk into my home. "You look beautiful by the way." He whispers into my ear then kisses me on the cheek as he brushes past me.

I wipe away his kiss and a sick feeling pools in the pit of my stomach. I look down at my loose t-shirt and short skin-tight cheer shorts I've managed to get on over my ass and regret my decision. I've been comfortable all day, but now I feel naked and vulnerable.

For a long minute, I stand there in shock just staring at him walking around my home as if he has every right to be here. No, just no.

"What are you doing?" I snap.

He stops walking around my living room and looks over at me, a disturbing look in his eye that sends a shiver down my back. "I thought we could talk about the misunderstanding from the other day."

"It's not appropriate for you to be here. Leave now."

He crosses his arms and gives me a smug grin. "Let's work this out like adults. You've made your point, now drop the charges so we can both go on about our lives like none of this happened."

I back away not wanting him anywhere near me. I back up against the fireplace and wrap my hand around the fire poker. "I didn't invite you in and I don't want you here. Get the hell out of my house before I call the police."

Continuing to walk towards me his nasty grin turns into a sneer and his eyes are full of malice. I grip the poker tightly ready to swing if I need to. "You're not calling anyone bitch." He growls, backhanding me in the cheek.

I fly into the fireplace, my back hitting the brick mantle. Motherfucker that hurts. I fall to the ground, the fire poker at my side, but just out of reach. Leaning over I try reaching for it, but my fingers are inches away.

"I tried to be nice and work this out." He says in a menacing tone as he reaches for my leg and pulls me in front of him.

I kick at him pushing myself closer to the poker, my fingers finally able to touch it. "Get away from me! I don't want this!" I yell. He laughs and chills run up and down my spine. When he reaches for me again, I swing the poker and almost miss, catching him against his cheek.

"You stupid cunt!" He yells grabbing for me again.

I roll to my stomach out of his reach and try to get to my knees. Wrong move. Dr. Hammond covers my back and pulls my arms behind me, holding them in one of his hands while the other reaches under me to fondle my breast. He pushes his erection against my ass and bile rises up my throat. I'm going to be sick. This can't be fucking happening to me, not again. I knew he was a creep, but I never thought this would happen.

One second Dr. Hammond is on top of me and the next he isn't. There's a crash behind me, then a gentle hand touches my shoulder. "Honey, it's Weston." Rolling over to my side I look up and see Weston crouching down in front of me. As soon as I see him, I start to cry, relieved that someone is here, and I didn't have to go through what was about to happen.

Weston stands and lifts me into his arms carrying me towards my front door. I look over and see Jackson beating the shit out of Dr. Hammond, kicking his curled up body over and over again.

"Jacks, that's enough man," Weston says as we pass him. "She needs you more than you need to kill him."

Jackson looks up and his golden eyes find mine. "Shit. Come here, love. He walks over to Weston and takes me from him then walks out of the house and to his truck with me in his arms. He opens the door and sets me in the driver's side seat then looks me over.

He runs his knuckles over my bruised cheek lightly and I flinch. Fire burns in his eyes and I know he wants to do more to Dr. Hammond.

"He's not worth it," I warn.

"He fucking put his hands on you for the second time Hannah! If we didn't get here when we did, who knows what he would have done! He's dead!" He shouts.

"What the fuck happened?" I hear Remington say from behind Jackson.

"It's a shit-show man," Weston says. "The guy who messed with her car, the same guy that hurt her at work, was attacking her in the living room when we got here."

"Fuck, is she okay?" Remington asks.

"I'm fine."

"You're not fine!" Jackson, Weston, and Remington all shout at once.

It's not the right time, but I burst out laughing. All three of them look about to hulk out and it's too much after everything that just happened. They all look at me like I've lost my mind and that only makes me laugh harder.

"I think she needs to see a doctor," Remington suggests, and finally my laughter stops.

"I'm not going to the hospital," I say, and Rem rolls his eyes at me.

"Why was he out of jail? I thought he was arrested two days ago."

Jackson who looks read to kill takes a deep breath. "Give me a minute to call this in."

"We're going to go keep an eye on the doctor," Remington says and walks into my house with Weston following.

I listen as Jackson calls his people to my house. Within ten minutes, two cop cars arrive, and an ambulance pulls up. The paramedics insist I get checked out, even though I only have some scratches and bruises. As I'm being questioned by the police in the back of the ambulance, holding an ice pack to my face, I watch two officers lead a handcuffed Dr. Hammond to one of the police cruisers. They put him in the back and drive away with him. When I've finished giving my statement to the police officers, they walk away with Jackson to talk to him. Weston joins them and Remington walks over to stand with me.

"I don't want to go to the hospital."

"Hannah, you know better than most. You should be checked over." Kyle, one of the paramedics I know from the emergency room says.

"Kyle, I know you're trying to help, but I'm not going. I'll sign whatever it is you need me to, but I'm not going to the emergency room."

"Either you go to the hospital your Jameson checks you out. Pick one but it's happening." Remington demands. Where is the goofy guy that cracks jokes every other sentence?

"Rem, come on."

"No. If you don't let Jameson check you over to make sure you're okay, I'll drive you to the hospital myself and sit with you until you've been seen."

"Fine. Jameson can do what he does best." I sigh. "Kyle give me the waiver please."

Kyle sighs and reaches for the waiver for me to sign. He fills out his part out and then hands it to me and points to where I need to sign. "Just sign right here."

I sign my name and he takes the paper back. "Come on Sis," Remington says, helping me out of the ambulance.

Jackson, who's been keeping an eye on me, says a few more words to the officers then shakes their hands. They get into their cruiser and drive off while Weston and Jackson walk back to where I'm standing with Remington.

"What did you mean when you said it was the same guy who messed with my car?" I ask Weston.

Weston looks at me then at Jackson and Remington. "I just assumed it was the same guy."

"Don't lie to me, Weston. The way you said it, you knew Dr. Hammond was the person who messed with my car. How?"

Weston looks at Jackson. Jackson sighs and dips his chin to his chest and closes his eyes before he looks back over at me. "Do you trust me, trust us?"

"Of course, I trust you all. What does that have to do with anything?"

"I promise to tell you everything you want to know, but I don't want to have this conversation here. Let's get you a bag packed, and we'll go back to the property."

"Why can't we talk here?"

"Love, I know you're full of questions, but you said you trusted me. Can you do this one thing for me and save your questions for later?"

Jackson looks as worn out and raw as I feel. My heart hurts for him and I just want to hold him and take away everything he's feeling. "Okay."

Jackson helps me pack an overnight bag with a couple of days' worth of clothes and my toiletries. I don't know where I'm staying or how long he expects me to be gone, but I promised him I'd save my questions for later. I don't know what's going on, but I do trust him and the Walker family.

CHAPTER 8

JACKSON

While Hannah packs, I quickly shoot off a message to the pack's group chat asking everyone to meet at my house in twenty minutes. I'm not willing to lie to Hannah and having Lillian there will make telling her the truth easier. This wasn't how I expected she would find out, but my hope is that having her best friend there will ease her into this way of life.

"I'm ready." She says as she zips up her duffle bag on her bed.

I grab her bag and walk out towards the front door where she grabs her purse and slings it over her shoulder. Weston and Remington already took off in Rem's truck so it's just us. She looks around the house then at me and smiles weakly. I hate that she had to go through this. If I were a few minutes earlier, it never would have happened.

Once she has closed and locked her front door I walk

to my truck and put her bag in the back seat. I expect to see Hannah walking to the other side of my truck to get in, but I'm surprised when I see her getting in her car.

"What are you doing?" I ask walking over to her.

"Getting in my car." She says giving me a questioning look.

"Hannah, please get in my truck. I'm not letting you drive right now after what just happened."

"No. What if I need to go somewhere? What about work?"

"We'll talk about you going back to work later. If you need to go somewhere, I'll take you wherever you need to go."

"You don't get to tell me what I do and don't do. I decide when I go to work. I decide! And I can drive my freaking car Jackson, I'm not broken." She huffs in annoyance.

Crouching down in front of her I take her hand and stare into her deep blue eyes. "Baby, no one said you were broken. You don't have to prove anything to anyone. You don't have to be strong right now."

We're in a standoff waiting to see who will cave first. She's doing everything she can to hold her head high and not look weak. Little does she know I'm the last person she needs to worry about feeling weak in front of. I want to be the man standing behind her, holding her up when things are hard. From the little I've gathered, she's had to rely on herself for a long time. "Hannah, someone just attacked you in your home. Let me take care of you. Let me be the one to shoulder your heavy."

She reaches her hand out and I take it, pulling her out of her car and to her feet. Handing me her keys, she leans into me as I close her door and lock it. Pocketing her keys, I realize she's given more to me than she might even know. She trusts me to take care of her, trusts me to be honest and has given me the time to do so. Down deep in her soul she knows that I'm her person, and that's everything to me.

I lead her around to the passenger side of my truck and help her in. Once she's buckled up, I sprint around to my side and get in, starting the truck to get us home. Hannah surprises me when she reaches across the console and grabs my hand. "Thank you, Jackson."

I bring her hand up to my lips and kiss it softly. "What did I tell you about saying thank you sweet girl?"

"That I don't have to?"

"That's right. You're mine now Hannah. Mine to care for, mine to protect, mine for always. I'm never going to let him hurt you again, not him or anyone else. I promise Hannah. I won't let you down again."

"You can't promise me that and I don't expect you to."

"Expect it."

With a small smile gracing her beautiful face, I pull out of her driveway and drive to the safety of my home. If I have it my way, she'll never sleep another night here again.

When we pull up my driveway, I see that my pack is already here.

Hannah looks around at all of the vehicles parked in front of my house. "Why is everyone here?" She asks.

"I thought it would be easier. Do you still trust me?"

"Yes." She says emphatically.

"Good. Now sit there and let me get your door."

Hannah rolls her eyes but sits still and waits for me. After grabbing her bag from the back seat, I circle around the truck and open her door. She looks nervous and I hate that she feels this way. Hopefully, this conversation doesn't go sideways like Jameson and Lillian's went.

When we walk into the house through the front door everyone is in the living room waiting for us. Lillian is sitting on Jameson's lap in one of the recliners. Remington and Hudson are sitting beside each other on the loveseat and Weston is standing in the corner of the room watching everyone.

Hannah gives a small wave to our pack. Yes, our pack, because she's a part of us now, and more importantly, a part of me. Setting her bag down, we walk hand in hand to the couch and sit down facing everyone.

"I'm okay. You guys can stop staring at me now."

Lillian smacks Jameson's hand and gets up from his lap to come and sit beside Hannah. She wraps Hannah in her arms and rubs her back. "I'm so sorry that happened Han. I'm so sorry." She tells her softly.

"It's okay," Hannah tells her best friend.

It is not okay, not in the least, and judging by everyone's face in this room they all agree. The bad doctor will get what's coming to him, but first, we need to take care of Hannah.

"So, who's going to tell me what's going on?" Hannah asks looking around the room. "What's the big secret we couldn't talk about at my house?"

Everyone looks at me. Seeing this, Hannah stares at me expectantly. "Well?"

"You've heard of shifters before, right?"

Hannah's brows draw together. "Shifters? Like a human turning into an animal?"

"Yes." We all answer.

She bursts into laughter. I'm starting to worry that maybe Rem was right, maybe she does need to go see a doctor.

"Hannah honey, why are you laughing?" Lillian asks, looking at her with concern.

"I'm sorry, all of you look so serious right now. Of course, I've heard of shifters. I know they aren't loud and proud like they used to be before the war, but they are still around."

"How do you know about the war?" Jameson asks her. The War of the Species isn't a secret, but it's also something most people don't talk about.

Hannah shrugs. "My cousin Willow is a fox shifter. Her mom, my mom's sister, mated to a fox shifter. When I would spend time over at their house my uncle Marc would tell us about the war and why it was important not to talk about Willow being a shifter."

"You know about mates?" I ask.

"Oh yes, I know all about them. Willow and I grilled her dad about it relentlessly when we were younger. I was always so jealous of the fact that she would one day meet the perfect man for her and just know immediately he was the one she got to spend the rest of her life with."

"If you need anything I'm right up the road or just a phone call away," Lillian says standing. "Come on guys, let's give them time to talk. They don't need us here for this."

"Wait. I don't get it." Hannah says, confusion clouding her beautiful face.

"You will darlin'," Hudson replies following Remington out of the house.

"Weston?" Hannah asks as he's about to walk out.

He stops. "You're in good hands. If you need anything, you let me know." He tells her, giving her a rare smile.

"Hold on, I'm going to examine Hannah before we leave," Jameson tells Lillian, then looks at me. "As long as that's still what you want."

"Thank you, Jameson. Yes please."

It takes all of five minutes for Jameson to examine Her and tell me what we already knew. She has a few cuts and bruises, but in a few days, she'll be healed up and feeling better.

Once they've all gone Hannah turns to me. "Well besides Jameson, everyone else was acting strange. I take it this has to do with shifters and mates."

I nod and gesture for her to sit back on the couch, which she does. "I'll start at the beginning. My brother, cousins, and I are all grizzly bear shifters-"

"Oh my god! It was you!" She shouts.

"It was me?"

"The other night, when I almost ran into a bear, it was you, right?"

A slow grin spreads across my face. "Yeah, it was me."

Hannah smacks my arm. "What the hell Jackson, I could have hurt you!"

I laugh. "I've never met a fox shifter before, but all of the other shifters I've met and know, heal quickly. I would have been fine I assure you."

"Oh yeah. It's the same for Willow too. One day when we were like seven or eight, we were climbing a tree and Willow ended up falling from a really high branch. I was freaking out. I felt so bad, I'm older than her by a year and a half and it was my idea to climb the stupid tree. So, I'm freaking out and we walk into her house both of us a blubbering mess. Long story short, she was fine the next day and I learned something new. Okay, go ahead. Sorry."

"Don't be sorry. When I was looking at your car the night it wouldn't start, I scented-"

"Because shifters have hella good senses." She mumbles to herself her eyes wide with understanding.

Chuckling, I nod. "Yes, we do. Weston and I both scented someone besides you around your car. Weston figured out that someone had put something in your gas tank and that's why your car was giving you issues. Suffice to say we thought it was the male who had been around your car. When we got to your place today it was Hammond that we scented on your car."

"What a fucker! I can't believe he messed with my car on top of everything else! I'm sure I'm not the first person he's done this to. There are so many rumors about how he comes onto the nurses. How is he still working at the hospital?"

"I have no idea, but I have my men looking into him right now. I told them to unearth every dirty secret they can on the fuck. When I go in tomorrow I'll know more."

"Good. I want him locked away for a long time. Not only for what he tried to do to me but what he has done to other women." Hannah takes a deep breath, visibly trying to calm herself down. "So why did I need to pack a bag?"

"For a few reasons. One, we don't know the kind of connections he has or when he'll get out on bail. He was set free on his own recognizance this morning. You should have been notified though. If he is let out again, I don't want you to be home alone."

"That makes sense. What are the other reasons?" She asks, her cheeks turning bright pink, her heartbeat picking up speed.

Lacing my fingers through hers, I hold her hand rubbing my thumb lightly across her pale skin. Looking down into her beautiful blue eyes I struggle with how to start or what to say. "Hannah, I could kick myself for all those times I missed a family night when you were here. So many months were wasted because of my own foolishness. This should have never happened to you and I can't tell you how sorry I am."

Hannah's brow furrows and she looks like she's about to say something, but I shake my head needing to get the rest of this out.

"You are my mate, Hannah. I knew the moment I scented you the night of the bonfire while I was running through the woods. That's why I came running through the trees and stopped in front of you. My bear wanted to meet you, but I held him back not wanting to frighten you. The second I stepped into the house and saw you I was done for."

CHAPTER 9

HANNAH

"I'm your mate?" I ask completely dumbfounded.

"Yeah, you are." He breathes out. His eyes are filled with so much... devotion, relief, desire, hunger. There's so much behind his golden eyes. The way he's looking at me makes my stomach flutter and my heart beat faster, but none of this makes sense. How can you meet someone and feel this much instantly?

"Are you sure? I mean, is there any way you could have gotten it wrong?" I'm kind of freaking out here, and Jackson the sexy man that he is, sits there cool as a cucumber giving me a devilish grin. I feel so unprepared for this. What am I supposed to say or do? Am I supposed to do anything? Does that mean what I'm feeling wasn't me, but because I'm his mate?

"There's no getting it wrong Hannah. You're mine and

I'm yours." He grins, double dimples donning his unshaven face.

I stand feeling lightheaded and uncertain. I've convinced myself for so long that love isn't something I would ever find, but here it is in front of me, mine for the taking. "I need to go lie down. Can you point me to my room?"

"Of course, you must be exhausted."

Pursing my lips together, I nod. It's a hell of a lot more than that, but yeah, lying down sounds like the best idea right now. I need to be alone.

Jackson stands and walks over to my bag and picks it up. He pauses at the stairs and looks down the hallway towards his room. After a moment he shakes his head and walks up the stairs. I follow behind him to the top where he pauses and looks back at me with an unsure smile. I try smiling back, but it's hard. Everything feels awkward between us now.

He turns left and walks into the first bedroom, putting my bag on the bed. "The bathroom is right through here." He says walking to one of the doors in the room and opening it.

"Thank you, Jackson."

"Always Hannah. I know we still have a lot to talk about, but we can do that later when you feel up to it."

I nod, wanting him to leave while at the same time wanting him to pull me into his arms and hold me forever.

"Make yourself at home. If there's anything you need

let me know and I'll be happy to get it for you. I was going to make some soup and sandwiches for dinner if you're up for it."

God, I'm such a bitch. He's trying so hard, being nothing but kind and supportive, and I just want to be left alone. "Soup and sandwiches sound amazing."

"I'll wait for you. Whenever you come down, I'll make them."

Jackson is about to walk out of the room, but before he leaves, he turns and steps up to me. He wraps an arm around my back holding me delicately and drops a kiss on the side of my head. "I know this is a lot to take in. We'll take this as slow as you need. I've waited over fifty years to find you, and I will wait however long you need. I'm always going to be here, even if you decide you don't want this, you don't want me, I'll be here."

Just the idea of not being in his life, not being his mate, stabs me in the heart. I bite my bottom lip, so I don't cry out in pain. Instead, I nod my head up and down. Hot tears well up in my eyes but I hold them back to keep them from falling.

He kisses me on my temple, holding his lips there for a couple of moments before he pulls away and walks out of my room. I stare down at the ground until I hear him walk out of the room and downstairs. As soon as I know he's gone and can't see me, I close the door and fling myself onto the bed sobbing.

I'm so confused right now. I want Jackson more than

anything, but it doesn't make sense. This sudden urge to have him around me at all times is so foreign to me. I've been on my own for years now, relying on myself for everything. When I was nineteen my grandmother passed away and my mom went on an extended trip out of the country. We were never really close, so when Gram passed, she had no reason to stick around. I'll hear from her every once in a while, but she's living her own life doing what makes her happy. I can't fault her for wanting that, but I long to have her around, especially at times like these.

When Jackson said I was his mate, I was shocked. Jameson and Lillian's relationship makes a whole lot more sense now. They are mates. Jameson must have known when Lillian came in off the ambulance. That must have killed him seeing his mate lying there half dead. Everything worked out though and they are living their life in pure bliss.

All I know about mates is what I've learned from my Uncle Marc. I watched him with my Aunt Tiffany and how he loved her. They were so in love and from what I saw, his devotion to her never lessened. I always thought she was lucky to be loved like that. Isn't this what I've always wanted? Did it happen this fast for her?

Grabbing my phone, I call my aunt.

"Hannah Banana, it's been a long time girl. How are you?" A deep but jovial voice answers.

"Hey Uncle Marc, is Aunt Tiffany there?" I ask.

"You sure you're okay? You don't sound right."

"I'll be okay. It's been a long day and I just need to talk to Aunt Tiffany about something."

He sighs. "You got it girl, one sec."

I hear him cover the phone and talk to someone, but I don't hear what he says.

"Hey honey, you okay? Marc says you don't sound good."

I laugh and a few tears fall, as soon as they start, I can't hold them back. "Oh honey, tell me what's going on. Do you need me to come down there?"

"No, no I'm going to be okay, I promise. Something bad happened today, but my friends saved me."

"Saved you? What the hell happened?" Aunt Tiffany asks sternly.

"This doctor I work with came to my house. I didn't even know he was coming, he just showed up. He pushed into my house and I didn't know what to do, and then he tried to... he tried to..." I can't get the words out.

"Son of a bitch, that motherfucker is dead. Do you hear me, Hannah, he's dead!" Uncle Marc shouts.

I wipe the hot tears from my face with the palms of my hands and take a shuddering breath. "Pretty sure my mate will beat you to it." I snort.

"Mate?" He and Aunt Tiffany ask at the same time.

"Yeah turns out I have a mate. He's a good guy, the brother of my best friend's mate."

"I didn't think there were shifters in Berkley Springs."

"How do you know?" I ask, curious how he'd know about that.

"Don't worry about it, honey. Are you sure he's a good guy? You don't have to mate him if you don't want to." Uncle Marc tells me.

"I don't?"

"Of course, you don't. If you choose to, you can walk away. It might hurt like hell, feel like a piece of you has been stolen, but you can do it."

"I didn't know I would be affected like that. Even thinking about us not being together, hurts."

"That's part of shifter magic. You'll never be able to change into... What is he?"

"A grizzly."

"Damn."

I laugh at my stunned uncle.

"Not many of them around these days. Is his last name Walker?"

"It is..." I say curiously.

"It's a damn shame. Their pack used to be huge, but after the war, they were torn apart. They've been through a hell of a lot. It makes sense that some of them would break away and look to settle somewhere new."

"Honey, you do whatever you feel inside. When I met Marc, I had no idea why I fell in love with him so fast but giving into it was the easiest thing I've ever done. Loving him was the best decision I ever made. Finding your mate is the greatest gift you can receive in life."

"Your aunt is right. Since the war, many shifters don't find their mates and they end up living their lives alone."

"Can't they mate with someone who isn't their mate?"

"It doesn't work like that. If someone has been destined for you, would you chance giving your body to someone else because you can't wait for the perfect person? Some shifters do it, but the majority won't."

"That makes sense I guess."

"Mating to a shifter is worlds apart from marrying a human. The love is stronger, the bond is unbreakable. He's not your dad honey. He'll never betray you." My aunt tells me.

"Because he can't?" I wonder, thinking its part of shifter magic.

"No, because he won't. You're the most important thing in his world and will be until he's no longer living. It's just the way it is. He'd rather feel pain for eternity than for you to go a day unhappy. Don't take advantage of his devotion and love, because you have it without question." Uncle Marc warns.

"Thank you, Aunt Tiffany and Uncle Marc. This is what I needed to hear."

"Give him the chance to prove he won't hurt you honey. Trust him to be that person you never thought you'd find."

A single tear falls down my cheek and I nod silently, then laugh when I realize they can't see me. "I will."

"Call us if you need us to come down there and take care of *things*." Uncle Marc tells me.

"That won't be necessary. I'm safe here. Oh, and tell Willow to answer my texts. She's been ignoring me lately."

"Ai yi yi, that girl. She's going through it lately. I'll light a fire under her ass and make sure she calls you." Uncle Marc says before telling me he loves me and hanging up.

Once I end the call, I lie here curled up in bed. My heart doesn't feel so heavy and my head doesn't feel as confused as before. I touch the place where Dr. Hammond hit me and wince, the spot is still tender to the touch. I don't even want to look at my back, I'm sure it's black and blue where I hit the brick. Today could have been so much worse than it was. Thank God Jackson and Weston showed up when they did. I tell myself I need a few more minutes, but my eyelids grow heavy.

CHAPTER 10

JACKSON

I couldn't help but listen to their conversation. I shouldn't have, but I did. My shifter hearing allowed me to listen to everything Hannah said, and I was able to make out most of what her aunt and uncle told her.

I'll have to reach out to them and extend my thanks. It does my heart good to know she has family in her corner that not only understands what she's going through but that she has people that are there for her. As my mate, she'll never be alone again, but the more family the better.

When her soft snores reach my ears, I pick up my phone and call my brother.

"How's it going man?" He answers.

"She's sleeping now."

"Good, she needs to rest. What she really needs is to be close to you. She'll heal a hell of a lot faster that way."

"Would be if I could, but she needed space."

"It's that bad?" Jameson questions.

I breathe out a heavy sigh. "I'm not sure. I overheard her talking to her aunt and uncle and they mentioned me not being like her dad. I can only assume that means he wasn't the best dad or husband to her mom. What the hell is wrong with men Jameson?"

"Maybe humans aren't lucky enough to know who the right person is, and they jump in with the wrong one. Who the hell knows?" He answers.

It's hard for me to relate to someone like that. Our father shows our mother every day how much he loves her, so do all the other mated couples I grew up with. "If you commit to someone, you don't one day decide they aren't enough for you and just leave."

"Let's play devil's advocate here. Say you have a child one day that grows up and picks a person to mate with. They pick wrong. Do you want them to stay with that person even if it makes them unhappy?"

"Fuck no. But they won't have that problem since they'll be a shifter and they will have a mate, they won't have to choose. I get what you're saying though."

"Makes you think. Our mates are human. They feel the mating bond, but they also have to rely on their human instincts to either trust us or not. If your mate was hurt in the past and doesn't trust men, that's something you'll have to deal with. You have to prove to her that you're not only her mate, that doesn't mean as much to her, but that you're never going to want another."

"How the hell do I do that?"

"That's the question, isn't it? My guess, love her. Love her and never give her a reason to think you don't."

"Well, that's fucking obvious Jay. Do you have any other good advice?"

He laughs like the asshole he is. "Just be there for her bro. She'll feel it and know it's true. Trust the bond."

"I know you're right, but it's hard when she'd rather be alone than by my side."

"Is that what she really wants?"

Fuck if I know. "I gotta go. I'm going to check in with the station to see what's going on with Hammond. I'll call you later."

"Let me know if you need anything. You know I have your back."

"Yep," I say and hang up.

Before calling the station, I walk upstairs and check on my sleeping mate. Her bag is still on the bed, so I grab it and put it on the ground against the wall. Grabbing one of the throw blankets my mom made me when I was a kid, I cover her up. Unable to help myself, I brush her strawberry blonde locks out of her face and stroke her cheek, loving the feel of her skin against my fingers. Damn, I got lucky with her. She's the most beautiful creature I've ever seen.

Not wanting to leave her, I force myself to pull away and leave. I close her door and go back downstairs to make the call.

"Berkley Springs Police Department, how can I help you?" Marge, our hard as nails seventy-year-old receptionist answers.

"Hey Ms. Marge, it's Lieutenant Walker. Can you patch me into the sergeant on duty?"

"Sure can. That doctor that was brought in hasn't shut up since he's been here. Keeps talking about suing the department for excessive force and getting you fired for not disclosing you're a police officer."

"What did he want me to do, show him my badge while he was attacking her?"

Marge chuckles. "Between you and I, you did right by her. He could have taken a few more and lived."

"Ah Ms. Marge, I don't know if I would have been able to stop myself. Hannah Finnigan is going to be my wife. He hurt her, if I had gone any longer, I wouldn't have been able to stop."

"Any man who does something like that to a woman deserves to have his dick cut off." She sasses.

"I couldn't agree more. Now can you patch me into the sarge."

"You got it cupcake."

A few moments later someone else picks up the line. "You've got Sergeant Peters."

"Derrick, it's Walker. Tell me where we're at with that fucker."

"He's been booked. He's already had his attorney in

here demanding he be released on something that was a misunderstanding."

"Misunderstanding my ass. That piece of shit would have raped her if we didn't show up."

"I hear you, man. He's not being released until he's arraigned, and the judge sets the bail."

"Good. Have you been able to dig any dirt up on him yet?"

"Not yet, but we're still looking into it."

"Shit. Don't stop looking, leave nothing unchecked. I'll be in tomorrow to go over it."

"See you then." He says and hangs up.

I turn the ballgame on and listen to it while I wonder what I need to do to convince Hannah. Not only that, once Hammond is released on bail, I can't have her on her own. She's going to hate what I'm about to propose to her, but I can't help it. I won't leave her exposed to potentially get hurt again. The next time he gets to her, he'll be ruthless. I wonder if she'd be willing to take a leave of absence from her job until he is taken care of, if not I'll need to call her supervisor. Fuck, she's going to hate me.

After a while, I hear her walking around upstairs. I wait a minute, wondering if she'll go back to bed or come down, but when I hear her door open, I get up and go to the kitchen to start dinner. I'm not a great cook, but I can heat up a can of tomato soup.

By the time she makes it downstairs I'm taking the bread out of the bag. "How many sandwiches would you like, two or three?" I ask looking over at her. She's changed into an oversized Cubs long sleeve t-shirt that goes past her ass and a pair of grey leggings. Her hair is up in a ponytail and she looks beautiful.

"Three? I can't eat three sandwiches!" She laughs.

"So, two then?" I grin.

"I'll have one, just one." She smiles, raising one finger up to me. "Can I do anything to help?"

"Actually, now that you ask, I have the perfect job for you," I tell her.

"Awesome... what do you want me to do?"

Walking up to Hannah, I put my hands on her shoulders and turn her around. Once she's facing the living room, I start walking her towards the couch. "Sit."

Hannah sits on the couch and crosses her arms across her chest. "I'm not a dog Jackson."

"Baby, you're beautiful and definitely not a dog. Want to find us something good to watch?'

"You sure you want me to decide what we're watching?" She asks, raising her brow and taking the remote I've handed her.

"Go for it. Put on whatever you want."

I'm a little nervous when I walk away and hear an evil laugh escape her lips.

A few minutes later I walk into the living room carrying a wooden cutting board with a steaming bowl of tomato soup and a grilled cheese sandwich cut in half diagonally on it.

"You're getting fancy on me now Lieutenant, next thing I know you're going to dazzle me with a chocolate snack pack."

I laugh and place the cutting board on her lap and kiss her on the top of her head. "I just might have a couple of those in the fridge." I wink.

"This looks and smells amazing Jackson," Hannah says sincerely with a soft smile on her face.

"Good, what can I get you to drink?"

"Do you have a Coke?"

"Does Cherry Coke work?"

"Is the grass green, is the sky blue, does the moon change sizes?"

"So that's a yes then?"

"That's a heck yes." She winks.

I throw my head back laughing. This girl is nothing short of amazing. She experienced something traumatic less than five hours ago and now she's sitting here cracking jokes.

By the time I've come back to sit beside her with my own cutting board food tray, we keep it fancy in this house, Hannah has put on Cold Case Files and has the episode paused, waiting for me.

"You sure you want to watch this?"

"Now who's the one with all the questions?" She asks and takes a spoonful of soup. She closes her eyes and smiles. "This soup is good. What did you do to it?"

"Hmm?" I'm so entranced with watching her eat, her

tongue darting out to lick the soup on her lips I miss her question.

"Why does this soup taste so good?"

I shrug. "Not sure. I just used the soup and added milk."

"I've never tried that before, I always add water."

She unpauses the show and we eat our dinner and watch the episode in comfortable silence. When I see that she's done I put my tray down on the ottoman in front of us and stack her tray on top, bringing our dishes back to the kitchen. When I get back out there I see that she's pushed the ottoman against the couch and has snagged one of the blankets from inside it. I love that she's taken what I said to heart and is treating this place like home, since one day I hope that's what she'll call it. I sit back in my spot to finish our episode and spend time with the woman who has quickly stolen my heart.

"I can't believe you like to watch this show. I figured you'd want to watch something girlie."

Hannah laughs. "I'm not really into 'girlie shows.' I'd rather watch this or Forensic Files. If I need more of a storyline, I'm a CSI, NCIS, or Criminal Minds kind of girl."

"Do you like to watch sports?" I wonder aloud.

Pulling the blanket away from her, she points to her shirt. "What do you think?"

I laugh. "You like the Cubs?"

"Obviously. You know for a police lieutenant I thought you'd be a bit more observant."

"I've been doing this a long time, maybe I've gotten rusty."

"How long have you been a cop?"

"I've been a cop since nineteen eighty-eight, so about thirty-two years."

"Holy shit! How old are you?"

"I'm turning fifty-seven this year."

"I mean I knew shifters aged well, but damn, you look like you're thirty."

"Age is just a number baby," I say and give her a wink, secretly hoping me being significantly older than her isn't a problem we can't overcome.

"It most certainly is," she says to herself.

By the third episode, Hannah is asleep, her head in my lap and her body curled up on the couch. While I'd love to sleep with her beside me, I want her to get a good night's rest. I stand with her in my arms and carry her upstairs to her room where I put her to bed.

CHAPTER 11

HANNAH

My eyes flutter open when a strange noise wakes me. My heart starts to beat fast and I wonder what woke me up. The room is dark, so dark I can barely see a few feet in front of me. I'm lying in bed naked when the bed dips behind me. His naked body presses against mine, his thick cock resting in the crevice of my ass.

"Mate," He rasps against my ear. Jesus, just the tone of his voice has my pussy wet and needy. "Are you ready to be mine?" He asks, stroking his knuckles lightly down my naked back, placing a kiss against the nape of my neck.

"Mmm."

He glides his hand over my hip and dips it between my thighs. I shift them, opening myself to him.

"Yes." I moan, my eyes rolling to the back of my head as he strokes two fingers between my lips. Lifting my leg, I drape it

over his behind me. Back and forth his fingers move, my wetness coating them as he circles my clit.

"You are mine. Mine." He growls before I feel the scrape of his canines and he plunges his fingers inside me.

I wake up in bed alone, my hand between my sticky thighs. Groaning, I realize it was just a dream. A good dream. A dream I've had every night since I've come to stay with Jackson. Last night after dinner, I tried to go further with him, but he stopped us when I started tugging at the button of his jeans. I got up and went to bed without saying good night, feeling too many emotions. Frustration, anger, hurt, really fucking horny.

It's been over two weeks since Hammond was arrested. Luckily the judge held him without bail, calling him a danger to the public. I couldn't agree more. He's been charged with attempted rape and aggravated assault. A court date hasn't been scheduled, but as long as he's in jail, I'm good with it, for now.

Jackson asked me to stay with him since I'm his mate. It's been wonderful getting closer to him. Every day he shows me what kind of man he is, and every day I'm struck by the vast differences between him and my dad.

We've talked in great detail what it would mean for us to be mated. That once he gives me my mate mark, we're bonded for life. I've got the impression he's worried that I'll regret my decision later on, but this couldn't be further from the truth. I'm ready for forever with this man, if only he'd give into me.

Screw it. I toss the blanket off me and get out of bed. I'm tired of waiting and all this awkward tension that's been building between us. Looking down I realize all I've got on is a pair of white booty shorts and a loose Cubs t-shirt, the shirt is so big that it hangs off one shoulder. Not exactly sexy, but if I went searching, I'd make a ton of noise and probably not find anything worth wearing. This is me in all my glory.

I run my fingers through my tousled hair and tiptoe downstairs trying not to make much noise. When I get to his door, I take a deep breath and step in. I freeze when I find Jackson sitting up in bed, a white sheet pulled up to his hips, his back flat against the headboard, and his golden eyes glowing in the moonlight trained on me.

"Come here, baby," he says in a deep, sleep roughened voice.

I can't take my eyes off of him as I inch closer. My mate is sexy with tribal tattoos running down his right shoulder and arm. His muscular arms and torso have me biting my lip. But it's the hungry look in his eyes that has my heart pounding, my stomach fluttering, and my pussy wet. For a split second I double guess myself.

"Get your ass over here. Don't you dare doubt how fucking sexy you are." He growls then whips the blanket away, showing me his thick cock bulging between his hand. "Do you see this?" He asks, stroking his hand up his shaft, a drop of precum wetting the tip.

Hell yes, I see it. I nod, words escaping me.

"It's for you, only for you. Now get over here and show me what had you making those sexy fucking sounds upstairs."

"You heard me?"

"I heard every moan out of your mouth, every stroke of your fingers against that wet pussy."

Standing at the side of his bed, I'm suddenly nervous. Not that I'm here with my mate, but that I've never done this before. Jackson pats the space beside him my eyes going from his hand to him. Ah hell. Lifting my knee, I crawl into bed and sit beside him. Where is the girl who woke up in the middle of a sex dream not ten minutes ago?

Jackson leans in close running his nose up the nape of my neck, inhaling my scent. "So. Fucking. Sweet." He says, dropping kisses up my neck after every word. The palm of his hand slides against my cheek and turns my face to his.

His eyes are drawn to my mouth and he slowly rubs this thumb across my bottom lip and groans. "There are so many things I want to do to this mouth."

"Okay," I rasp, licking my lips.

Jackson groans and leans down, capturing my lips in a kiss that turns my world upside down. I curl my hand around his neck holding him close. Within seconds, Jackson grabs my hips and is lifting me on top of him, his bulging shaft hard against my pussy. It's not enough, I need more. I move over him, back and forth, rubbing my wet pussy against his cock, the head hitting my clit sending pleasure throughout my body.

"Jackson, I need more. I need all of you. Please..." I moan.

"Never. You never have to beg me for what is rightfully yours mate." He moves so fast, flipping me over so my back is lying against the bed and he's hovering over me, his golden eyes staring into my own. "Do you understand?"

"Yeah."

Jackson grabs my panties and slides them down my legs and tosses them to the side. He glides his hands over my ankles and up my calves, ever so slowly, teasing me with his touch. I part my knees when his hands slide behind and over my thighs as he pulls me down the bed closer to him. Leaning over me, his shaft resting against my wet pussy, he kisses up my stomach. He slowly moves my shirt up and sucks a hard nipple into his mouth.

I moan and writhe beneath him, his tongue circling my nipple and sucking again. I pull my shirt over my head and toss it aside watching his tongue circle around my other nipple. He slides his shaft through my lips, over and over, faster and faster. Reaching between us he lines his dick up at my center and looks up at me. I nod slightly and he pushes inside me, his thick girth stretching me tight.

"Ohh, Jackson, don't stop," I sigh.

"Never." He pants. "Fuck you're tight, so fucking tight, so fucking good." He moans and bottoms out inside me. Staring into my eyes, he grabs each of my hands lacing his fingers through mine, rests them near my head, and kisses me. Pulling out of me slowly, he thrusts inside me over and over, never stopping.

"I'm so close." I cry as he thrusts into me faster and faster.

"Me too, fuck. I love you, Hannah." He groans then bites down on my shoulder, fucking me through the pain, until pleasure replaces it and something magical happens. It's as if something tangible links us together, an unimaginable bond between his soul and mine. Intense pleasure courses through me just as Jackson reaches between us and rubs my clit and my orgasm consumes me. He continues to pummel in and out of me, until he thrusts in deeply and groans in satisfaction, filling me full of his hot cum.

We lay there still connected, panting, staring into each other's eyes. *I love him. I love him so fucking much it hurts.* He smiles, the kind of smile that reaches in and takes hold of your heart. That's when I hear him. *I love you too baby. God, I love you. You have no idea how much.*

I gasp when I realize what happened. "Really?" I ask aloud and laugh.

Jackson winks. "Yeah baby, really."

JACKSON

"Hey, baby?" I holler down the hall.

Hannah peaks her head out of the bedroom "Yeah?"

"Lillian's water just broke. Jameson needs us there as soon as possible," I tell her, grabbing my shoes to pull them on.

A few minutes later, Hannah comes rushing out of our bedroom holding her scrubs in her hands still wearing her pajamas and crying. I pull her into my arms and hold her while she cries.

"What's wrong baby?" I ask, starting to worry.

"They don't fit!" She cries.

Pulling away, I look down at my wife and then at the scrubs she's thrusting towards me. "Your clothes?" I ask.

She nods. "I can't wear them anymore. What am I

supposed to do now?" She sniffles as I wipe the tears from her face with the pads of my thumbs.

"We can order you bigger ones." I offer, thinking of the logical next step.

Hannah glares at me. "I don't want BIGGER ones!" She yells and starts pacing in front of me.

I hold up my hands in defeat. My wife is five months pregnant with our daughter and she already looks like she's close to popping. "I'm sorry."

She stops and looks at me. "Why are you apologizing?"

"Because I have absolutely no idea what you want me to say to make you happy, and it's killing me."

Her sour face instantly softens as she walks into my arms. "I'm sorry, I shouldn't have yelled at you."

"It's okay baby."

"No, it's not. I'm just so frustrated that none of my clothes fit. I'm so uncomfortable in my own body and it's driving me crazy."

"Is there anything I can do to make it better?" I ask.

"Just love me." She sighs into my chest.

I grin and rub my hand over the back of her head. *I'll always love you, baby. Nothing in this world could ever change that.*

Hannah looks up at me and stands on her tiptoes to give me a kiss, I meet her halfway and seal my lips against hers. *That is exactly what I needed to hear.*

Hannah walks back into our bedroom and comes out

five minutes later wearing a pair of jeggings and one of her old long sleeve Cubs shirts.

"Ready?"

"Ready. Let's go deliver some babies." She says walking to the front door.

Jameson and Lillian made the decision to deliver their twins at home as to not raise any suspicion. They also asked Hannah to be there to assist with the delivery as well as our mom, since she had gone through delivering a shifter baby before.

Mom and Dad have been staying at Hudson's house for the past week in preparation for the arrival of the babies. They were prepared to stay for the next couple of months but came early since shifter pregnancies tend to only be seven months. Guess human/shifter pregnancies are the same time frame, or they came early because they were twins... who knows.

Meeting Hannah at the door, I pull her into my arms and give her a long kiss. "You are beautiful, mate. Even more so now that you have our daughter growing inside you." I tell her rubbing my hand over her baby bump.

By the time we get to Jameson's, Lillian is in active labor.

Ten years later
HANNAH

Things around here are a lot of the same but in an incredible way. Jackson is now the sheriff in Berkley Springs, and I work part-time at a doctor's office in town while the kids are in school. That's right, after our daughter Jenna was born, I was pregnant with her little brother Jack within six months. Having two kids back to back was hard, but the pack was there to help whenever we needed it. Weston did a lot of babysitting in the early days. When Jenna was six, I found out I was pregnant with our last child, Jillian. While Jenna is quiet and book smart, her sister is a wild child, running around outside whenever we let her. Jack is our most relaxed and kind-hearted child. It's crazy how different they all are.

The pack has continued to grow by leaps and bounds since I was made a part of it. My cousin Willow came to town shortly before I gave birth and never left. That's a story for another time though, just like the rest of the Walker men.

Remington's book is up next. Be sure to stick around to find out who his mate is and the crazy journey they must take to get to their happily ever after. Just like Jameson and Jackson, he'll do whatever it takes to keep his woman, even if it means becoming someone he never thought he'd be.

REMINGTON

VIOLET SPENCER

I fucked up.

Would you call quitting your job on the spur of the moment a mistake? Same girl, same, but that's what I did. It wasn't a smart move since I have next to nothing in savings. Nope, definitely wasn't one of my finest moments. Hence, I fucked up last night.

Let me paint you a picture so you can understand why I couldn't keep my mouth shut. It was eight forty-five, and I was about to lock up and go home for the weekend. I was exhausted after the week from hell. The day had been long, the three girls I have working for me were cranky, I wouldn't be surprised if their periods were synced at this point, and the kids, well the kids were hellions. Suffice to say, everyone needed the weekend off to recuperate and get our heads back in the game.

It was the first week without Lillian since she quit due to her pregnancy. I was happy for her, I really was, but It was awful for us. I'm the director of Sunnytime Daycare and Preschool and the owner refused to let me hire another teacher to replace Lillian. The evil witch told me I would have to teach the class instead. It wasn't that I couldn't teach pre-kindergarten, I have the certifications, but I don't have the time on top of everything else I have to do to run the center. The week from hell didn't look like it would get better anytime soon.

My hand was on the door, my purse was slung over my shoulder, heavy with curriculum books, and then the phone rang. I should have let the call go to voicemail, but my conscience got the better of me and I picked it up. I shouldn't have done it. I knew it the moment I heard Catherine's screeching voice cut across the line.

"What took you so long to answer the phone?" She snapped before I had the chance to say hello.

"It only rang once," I said curtly.

She scoffed and I could picture her looking down at me with that look of disdain on her face I often see when she comes to visit. "Violet, I've been going over last month's paperwork and you screwed it up, again."

I took a deep breath as I remembered the hours I spent

making sure I did everything the way she liked it. It wasn't that I did it wrong, it's that it wasn't how she wanted it. "I did everything the way you told me to and double-checked it before I sent it off. What is wrong with it now?" I asked, finally allowing my frustration to bleed into my words.

"What is wrong? Are you kidding me?" She screeched. "How dare you speak to me that way. I should have fired you months ago. You're an incompetent worker and a sorry excuse for a daycare director."

"Excuse me?" I burst out, unable to contain my anger any longer. I've endured months of her verbal abuse, for the sake of my job.

She laughed coldly. "You have no idea what the hell you're doing. I told my husband we should fire you the moment we bought the place last year, but the fool said you would be fine. You have been nothing but a letdown. I wouldn't doubt it if you sat on your fat ass all day on the internet while the idiots you hired do nothing but play on their phones."

"Fuck you." I said, and before she could fire me, I added, "I quit."

"Ex-" Click.

That was about all I could handle of that conversation. With my palms flat against the desk, I hung my head in defeat, sighing deeply. For months I've been doing nothing but bending over backward for Catherine trying to make her happy, but nothing was ever good enough for her. I had been the director of Sunnytime Daycare and

Preschool for two years before the Millers bought it from the old owners. The previous owners never had a problem with how I ran things, ever! It doesn't help that Catherine has no idea how to actually run a daycare. Sure, she has a degree in early childhood education, but she's never used it. She's just a bored housewife who asked her husband to buy her a daycare to run so she would have something to do while he was busy at work. At first, she thought it was fun to come in and spruce the place up, change everything around, and then tell me how to do my job.

I'd had enough. I grabbed everything that was mine off of my desk and stuffed it into an empty paper box. Then I set the alarm, turned out the lights, and walked out of the center, locking up behind me. I stared down at the keys in my hands for a long moment. What was I supposed to do with them now? I guess I'll have to bring them in on Monday when it's time to open.

That's when it set in that I no longer had a job. The job that I needed. I went home and changed into my comfiest clothes and drowned my sorrows in a large pepperoni, olive, and mushroom pizza and a bottle of red. I worried all night about the girls who still worked there and the children I wouldn't see anymore. What had I done?

When I woke up this morning my head was throbbing and I felt worse than ever about last night. Regret isn't a word I believe in, knowing that everything happens for a reason. That being said, I'm pissed at myself for acting so rashly. I had fucked up bad and I didn't know what to do about it. I wish I could have bought the daycare from the previous owners when they were ready to sell, but I was only twenty-six and had no idea what I was getting myself into or how to even go about getting a loan to buy a business.

The first thing I do after brewing a cup of black coffee and swallowing four ibuprofen is to look at my checking and savings account. I cringe. Nope, shouldn't have done that. "Fuck my life." I groan pushing my laptop away from me.

Instead of dwelling on the mess I've made, I decide to get out of the house and go for a hike to clear my head. I take a hot shower that wakes me up and puts me in a little bit of a better mood. Once I'm out I shake out my shoulder-length wavy black hair and pull it into a bun. I put on some black leggings, a lime green muscle shirt, and my tennis shoes. I grab my camera and shove it into a backpack with a couple of waters and some granola bars and goldfish. I drive to the state park in hopes that a long hike through the forest is just what I need to help me figure out what I'm going to do next.

The day is beautiful with the sun shining through the dense trees and a slight breeze. I hike deep into the forest and eventually end up pulling out my camera, taking several shots of the beautiful scenery. When I was a kid I used to wish I could live in my treehouse in the middle of the forest. How cool would it be to wake up to this every morning?

Eventually, I come across a twenty-foot waterfall flowing into a nice sized pond that would be perfect for swimming. It's hot out and I'd love nothing more than to explore how deep the water goes. Instead, I take off my shoes and socks and dip my feet into the surprisingly cold water and take some shots of the waterfall. Resting with my hands behind me, my palms flat in the soft grass, I tilt my head back to feel the warm sun against my skin. I sit here for a while listening to the sounds of nature and wish that this could be my life.

How had everything gotten so screwed up? That's right, it was my damn mouth. Daddy always said I needed to keep it shut or the devil was liable to come out. I roll my eyes thinking about my dad and all of his off the wall sayings. He and mom moved down to Florida where it's warmer. I've been down to visit and there's no way in hell I want to end up living in that lawless swamp. Heaven help me, but I'll do anything, except beg for my job back, before moving down there with them.

After a while, I put on my socks and shoes to make my way back to my car. At least that is my intention. After about an hour of walking and not seeing anything that looks familiar, I realize I'm lost in the forest that just a few hours ago put my troubled mind at ease. When I was little, my dad would bring me out here and we would go for hikes, but it's been over ten years since I've been back and nothing looks the same.

I've been lost for over two hours when panic sets in.

Leaning against a tall pine tree, I knock my head against the trunk. "Think... think... think." I murmur. Why am I whispering to myself? It's not like anyone can hear me. That's when I hear my phone beep for the first time in hours. It's an email notification and I immediately think it's a scathing message from Catherine. I shake my head knowing I won't want to read that. Wait, my phone has a map app. I wonder if it will help me find my way. I mean as long as I get reception way out here, it should get me where I need to go. I pull my phone out of my backpack and see that there isn't much battery life left. I was smart enough to bring water and some snacks, but not smart enough to charge my phone before coming out into the unknown. I tap on the map app hoping to find myself and a way back to the parking lot.

"Yesss!" I cheer and jump up and down when the app pinpoints me somewhere in the state park. I zoom in and see that I'm not too far from the parking lot, but I'm definitely off the beaten path. I start walking in the direction that the arrow points on my app and can't believe my good luck. I'm looking down at my phone, not paying attention to what's in front of me as I make sure I'm going the right way. As soon as I take the step I know it's too late to back up, I'm already falling. This would be the cherry on the fucking ice cream sundae of my life. I think to myself as I descend to the ground, eyes squeezed shut. As soon as my body hits the ground I scream out in pain. I'm pretty sure my leg isn't supposed to twist that way. Every second that passes the pain shooting through my leg, and the rest of my body, gets stronger and harder to handle. I try rolling to the side but the only thing that does is make everything hurt worse. Trying to keep still, I steady my breathing as much as I can. Getting up isn't an option. Everything hurts. My head, my back, my arms, my legs. Everything. I lie here, staring up at the tops of the trees for what feels like hours. Little by little it's harder to keep my eyes open and stay alert. Eventually, I succumb to my needs and close my eyes.

Elisa's Elite Readers

Psst!
All the good stuff
happens in my reader group!

xoxo.

Elisa

ABOUT THE AUTHOR

Elisa Leigh writes dirty talking alpha men who are rough, possessive, and totally in love with their women. Elisa promises with every book she writes, to give you a sometimes sweet and always steamy love story that will end with a Happily Ever After!

Signup for her newsletter HERE

Visit www.elisaleigh.com for current releases and book updates.

All books in series are listed in reading order. All books are on Amazon and free on Kindle Unlimited.

Diablo Sinners MC

Nixon

New Hope Shifters

Jameson

Jackson

Remington - coming soon

Hudson - coming soon

Winston - coming soon

Panthera Security

Finally, Our Forever

Keeping Our Forever (MMF)

Fighting Our Forever (MFM)

Book 4 Cash Owens - coming soon

Book 5 Adam Kingston - coming soon

Steel Daggers MC (Series Complete)

PRES

ROCK

RASH & JESTER (MMF)

PRINCE

TRITON

CARTER

Daddy Knows Best co-written with MK Moore

Daddy Captain

Daddy Lawyer - coming soon

Black Hills Shifters written with M.Merin

Cole's Salvation - Book 1

Ruby's Strength - Book 3

Clearwater Curves Novella Series

Sweet Curves

Forever Safe Romance Series

Loving Summer Co-Written with MK Moore

Sweet Love

Curvy and the Beast Co-Written with MK Moore

Forever Safe Christmas

Sleigh Me Baby

A Queen For Christmas Co-Written with MK Moore

<u>Falling on the Fourth</u>

Red, White, & Mine - Book 3

<u>Thankful for The Jones Sisters</u>

Falling for Sadie Mae - Book 3

<u>Seven Brides of Christmas</u>

The Bride's Christmas Miracle

A Bride for Theo

<u>A Hauntingly Romantic Halloween Series</u>

Hunting Lucy - Book 4

<u>The Whelan Brothers</u>

The Irishman - Book 1

<u>Standalones</u>

**All of these are book 1 in a series. Book 2 in the series are coming soon.

His Curvy Woman

Owning Madison

His Curvy Witch

Holding Onto Kinsley

Roped Into Love

Their Virgin Valentine

Bishop (Part One)

ACKNOWLEDGMENTS

I just want to give a big shout out to Ashley Lewis at Geeky Girl Review Cafe, Geeky Girl Whole Latte Books, and Geeky Girl Author Services. Thank you for being an amazing friend. You're doing amazing supportive things and I couldn't be happier for you!

Jenny thank you so much for always checking in and being there to hop on read what I've added. You are an amazing beta reader and this book would definitely not be what it is without your help.

My beta reader team (Ashley, Jennie, Jenny, and Lola) you girls are amazing! Thank you for beta reading and helping to make my books what they are.

MK Moore thank you for your friendship and supportive words! I love you girl!

My ARC team thank you for reading and reviewing

Jackson. I hope you loved reading Jackson and Hannah's book as much as I loved writing it.

If you loved Jackson, please consider leaving a review on Amazon, Bookbub, or Goodreads. Every review, long or short, helps an author out.

xoxo,

Elisa